DANGER IN THE RING

Rosalie was raised on a farm in rural Italy by her mother and uncle. But her parent and guardian die within months of each other when she is just fourteen, and her future is uncertain — until she is rescued by her father, Drago, who invites her to join his exciting travelling circus. Though promised fame and fortune, disillusionment soon follows for Rosalie, and she finds herself living with another guardian, Drago's wealthy Uncle Angelo. Then, on the eve of her sixteenth birthday, she realizes that there are sinister forces at work in this family, and she must flee Sicily . . .

Books by Heather Graves
Published by Ulverscroft:

FLYING COLOURS
RED FOR DANGER
STARSHINE BLUE
EMERALD GREEN
INDIGO NIGHTS
ON TRACK TO MURDER
RIDING THE STORM

HEATHER GRAVES

DANGER IN THE RING

Complete and Unabridged

ULVERSCROFT
Leicester

First published in Great Britain in 2016 by
Robert Hale
an imprint of The Crowood Press
Wiltshire

First Large Print Edition
published 2017
by arrangement with
The Crowood Press
Wiltshire

A catalogue record for this book is available
from the British Library.

ISBN 978–1–4448–3407–9

Published by
F. A. Thorpe (Publishing)
Anstey, Leicestershire

Set by Words & Graphics Ltd.
Anstey, Leicestershire
Printed and bound in Great Britain by
T. J. International Ltd., Padstow, Cornwall

Prologue

Sicily 1969

Dante took off his hat and wiped his sweating forehead with his arm. Having been out since daybreak, checking row after row of his father's vines, he and his horse were both tired. Having satisfied himself that the vineyard was thriving and showing no evidence of pests or disease, he headed for home. Knowing that if the right weather continued there would be an excellent crop this season, he was looking forward to bringing his father this welcome news. Too ill to ride out and see the vineyard for himself, Alfredo Marino had to rely on his younger son's frequent reports. Although the old man's mind was as sharp as ever, his body was failing; each day he seemed to diminish a little more, the skin stretching ever more tightly across his cheekbones as he fought against the increasing pain. Death could not be far away as a full-time nurse had been engaged to look after the old man now.

Much as Dante loved his father, he couldn't help wondering what might happen

1

after his death. As his older brother never ceased to remind him, he was only the second son and with no real claim on the vineyard that presently provided a living for all of them. If tradition were to be followed, his elder brother, Alberto, must inherit the lot. Alberto, who showed little interest in the day-to-day activities of the farm and had long resented his brother's place in the old man's affections. When his father died, Dante knew Alberto was unlikely to keep him on, even as a farm manager, once the property fell into his hands. He would have to find something else to do with his life.

Before attending to his own needs, Dante left his weary horse with the stable boys, urging them to reward the animal with a rub-down and a good feed. Only then did he make his way to the kitchen at the rear of the farmhouse, looking forward to a late breakfast or an early lunch. On the way, he stopped in his tracks and groaned, recognizing Alberto's new Porsche parked carelessly across the driveway. He wasn't in the mood for a sparring match with his brother today.

Much as he expected, Alberto had made himself comfortable in the big farmhouse kitchen, leaning back in a chair, drinking coffee and smoking, his feet resting on the table. He hadn't even bothered to remove his shoes. Dante hadn't seen his brother for some time as he visited rarely, preferring to live in Messina with his long-suffering wife, but he could see at a glance that Alberto looked bloated and overweight, his eyes bloodshot and the buttons of his shirt straining across his ample belly.

'Morning, bro,' he said as he went in, closing the door carefully behind him. 'What brings you out here today?'

'Oh, I'm just here to check up on my inheritance.' Alberto's smile didn't quite reach his eyes. 'Nice to find you working so hard on my behalf, little brother. Might even keep you on when the old man croaks. Lord, but he's stretching it out, isn't he? Thought he'd be gone by now.'

Dante took a deep breath and closed his eyes. He would not lose his temper with Alberto today, although he knew his brother was angling for it.

At that moment his father's nurse, Pia, came into the kitchen; a slight, fair-haired girl, she managed to be beautiful even without the enhancement of make-up. It had been a relief to Dante when she joined their household where there had been no woman in charge for years, not since the death of his mother when he was a small boy. It was nice to have someone around who cared about clean linen and clothes. He had liked Pia from the outset with her good-humoured, 'no nonsense' ways and it felt good to be able to leave his sick father in such capable hands.

Ignoring Alberto, whose hungry gaze was raking her body, she spoke directly to Dante instead.

'I'm glad you're back early.' She smiled at him. 'Your father wants to see you, soon as poss.'

'Ooh, the favoured child,' Alberto mocked. 'Put lunch on hold, bro. Better not keep his lordship waiting — it might be too late.'

This last remark was one step too far for Dante who turned on him. 'Have you no love for our father at all? No concern for the pain that he suffers?'

'Who could love anyone that old?' Alberto shrugged. 'Outstayed his welcome, hasn't he? Bits dropping off even as we watch. The sooner he goes, the sooner the rest of us can get on with our lives.'

Dante glanced at Pia who shook her head, pushing him into the hall before things got physical or he could say any more. 'Don't rise to the bait, Dante. Upsetting people is how that man gets his kicks. Take deep breaths now. You don't want to go in to your father with steam coming out of your ears.'

'I'd like to punch Alberto into the middle

of next week,' Dante muttered.

'Wouldn't we all?' Pia's smile was wry.

Inside the sick room, Dante found his father freshly washed and propped on a mountain of snowy white pillows. Pia was doing a good job. He drew up a chair to the old man's bedside and took the cold, gnarled hands into his own warm ones, as if he would transmit some of his youth and strength to his father.

'Alberto's downstairs.'

'Oh, I know.' Alfredo's voice wasn't strong but Dante could hear him well enough. 'Let's hope he stays there. I've no wish to see him. Thank you, Pia,' he said, dismissing the nurse. 'Will you see that we're not disturbed?'

'I'll sit right outside. Just ring if you need me.' Pia smiled before closing the door behind her.

'Good girl that,' Alfredo said. 'Knows how to keep her mouth shut, too.'

'That sounds like a conspiracy, Pop. What are you up to?'

'I'm tied to this bed and can't go anywhere, as you know. She has to do it all for me. Even fetched the lawyers here for me, too.'

'What did you need them for?'

'You're a good boy, Dante.' Alfredo withdrew a hand to rest it on his son's dark, curly head. 'My true heir who deserves a lot

5

more than the crumbs from Alberto's table. Aside from Pia and the lawyers of course, you'll be the first to know. I've sold the farm.'

'You've done what?' Dante sat back to stare at him, wondering if the illness had affected his father's judgement, after all.

'Don't worry, I'm still in my right mind. I sold it to cousin Florian.'

'Well, if you had to sell it to anyone, it makes sense. His vineyard runs next to ours. But Florian's always broke. Where did he get enough money to buy you out?'

'He's always coveted our lands, as you know. And a few months ago, he won a big lottery prize. Didn't tell anyone as he didn't want his wife's relatives coming round with the begging bowl.'

'They're the least of our worries. What about Alberto? He'll be furious — '

'So he mustn't find out until after I'm gone. Florian's sworn to secrecy, too. He won't say anything.'

Dante blew out a long breath. 'All hell will break loose when he does. And I hate to ask at a time like this, Pop, but what am I going to do?'

'Don't worry — I've taken care of all that. You're still young and unmarried, aren't you? There's no special girl?'

'No, Pop, there isn't.' Dante looked away,

reminded of the American girl he'd been crazy about some six months ago. He had even asked her to marry him.

She had laughed in his face, rejecting his impulsive proposal. 'Of course I can't marry you, Dante, because I'm a realist. You're a lovely man and it would be so easy to fall in love with you but I can't. If you had more to offer, I'd take you like a shot. But I refuse to struggle through life as my parents did, always in debt and wondering where the next dollar was coming from. That's why I'm splashing out on that Mediterranean cruise. I need to meet someone with money — I don't even care if he's old.'

This rejection allowed Dante to realize that his heart wasn't broken at all and he had, in fact, had a lucky escape. So, in answer to his father's question, he shook his head. 'I won't have any ties here — not after you're gone.'

Alfredo reached for his oxygen mask and took a deep breath from it, before going on. 'You will go to Australia. There are many Italians living in and around Melbourne. Most of my money is already there in a bank account in your name.'

'Hold on, Pop, you're going too fast for me. I can't possibly leave you here all alone — not before — '

'It won't be for long. I'm on borrowed time

now. Pia has promised to stay and look after me till the end. You must go; I don't want you sitting here, waiting for me to die. Alberto will find out what I've done soon enough and he'll — '

'Sounds as if you're afraid of him.'

'Of Alberto himself, no. He's a weakling, incapable of running his own life or taking any responsibility. But I'm very much afraid of his — associates. He fell in with a bad crowd. I don't know the whole story but they're into drug-dealing — organized crime — anything that will bring easy money.'

'How stupid can he be? Once you fall in with such people, they'll never let you escape.'

'Exactly. But it's dangerous to speak of such things, even behind closed doors. Have you never wondered how he manages to live so well? Running around in that sports car? He's no businessman.' Alfredo's voice was deep with scorn. 'I didn't work hard all my life to leave money for him to squander. But we're wasting time, speaking of that loser. Pass me that folder.' Alfredo pointed to some papers on his desk and Dante brought them to him. 'Those are your banking details. Keep them safe. Here are your travel documents, including a new passport.'

Dante looked through the package and

raised questioning eyes to his father. 'But, Pop, you're sending me to Australia by sea. It'll take forever.'

'Certainly. Gives you some time to get used to it all. If Alberto or his associates get wind of this, they'll be expecting you to travel by air.'

Dante's eyes widened. 'You think they'd come after me?'

'Without doubt. If they knew where you were. With the help of the lawyers, we're setting a false trail. Alberto will believe you've gone to the UK.'

Dante sat back and sighed, shaking his head. 'It's no good, Pop. I can't do it. I can't leave you here, helpless and alone.'

'What can they do to me now? Smother me with my own pillows?' Alfredo tried to laugh and had a coughing fit instead. 'It would be a blessed relief. Kiss me now and go with my blessing. Pia will take care of everything else.'

Less than a week later, armed with several courses to help him learn English on the month-long journey to Australia, Dante was on his way. The ship had scarcely left the Mediterranean when he received a telegram from Pia to say that his father had died peacefully in his sleep. He was alone in the world but with money enough to buy or create a business for himself; the choice would be his. He wondered what that American girl would think of him now and was pleased to discover that he didn't care.

★ ★ ★

Unused to having time on his hands, Dante had little to do on the long journey to Australia except make friends. The easy option would have been to spend time with fellow Italians but, anxious to improve his vocabulary before arriving in an English-speaking country, he struck up a friendship with Jimmy Halloran, a young Australian around his own age, returning home from his European tour. Dante needed to find out as much as possible about the country that was to be his new home.

Jimmy told him his father kept a small but successful racing stables on a place called the Peninsula, not far from the city of Melbourne. The boys soon discovered they had much in common, including that they shared the same birthday in early December.

'You just have to be a horseman,' Jimmy said. 'I won't believe you, if you say you can't ride.'

'Of course I can. I rode out almost every day, checking my father's vineyard.'

'And what are you going to do when you get to Australia?'

Each day, Jimmy would ask the same question and Dante would mutter something non-committal in return. It was becoming obvious to him that life in Melbourne or Victoria was going to be very different from the life he had known in Sicily. Finally, when they were crossing the Australian Bight just days away from Melbourne, Jimmy asked yet again and Dante finally told him about the inheritance waiting for him in Melbourne.

'So to honour my father's memory, I think I should carry on his tradition of wine-making and do what I know best,' Dante said. 'I'll buy enough land to start a small vineyard and — '

'That's what I thought you'd say.' Jimmy held up a hand for silence as Dante drew breath to argue. 'Please, hear me out first. Aside from the difficulty of getting good vines in commercial quantities, Australians aren't wine drinkers. Eventually, they'll catch up but that time isn't yet. Wine-making is still a cottage industry with Italians keeping a few vines at home to cater for themselves. Australia, for the most part, is a nation of beer drinkers and gamblers.'

'Oh, great.'

'No. I don't mean that quite as it sounds. I

11

should say we're an optimistic, happy-go-lucky people. Our favourite saying is 'she'll be apples, mate', meaning that we expect everything to turn out well. And horse racing has become a large part of *our* tradition — *our* heritage.'

'I see. Well, I'm beginning to, anyway.'

'Think about it, Dante. People say no meeting is ever by chance. We've lived in each other's pockets for almost a month now and I think you believe in our friendship as I do. You must know I want only the best for you.'

'Of course, Jim. As I wish the same for you.'

'Then I have a proposition for you. Why don't we start a horse racing stables and become trainers together? My dad's always saying he wants to expand; he'll put up the same as you and we'll be equal partners in a new venture. It'll be great fun and we'll make money together, I know.'

'It does sound exciting, Jim, but your father and I haven't met. And on the other hand, I don't know Australia and what it will be like to live there — not yet. And another thing, I don't know how far my money will take us. You must realize I can't say yes to all this without seeing the place and getting proper advice.'

'Take all the time you need.' Jim grinned,

slapping him on the shoulder. 'I just know it's going to work out.'

★ ★ ★

And it did. Unlike most friendships that spring up on holiday, the two young men became even firmer friends when Jimmy reached home territory. And when Dante met Jimmy's sister, Maureen, he fell in love. Really in love this time. There was a huge wedding and the older Hallorans welcomed him into the family, treating him like another son. Their new racing stables near Cranbourne on the outskirts of Melbourne went from strength to strength and when Maureen at last presented him with Leo, their first and only child, Dante could wish for no more. His happiness was complete.

1

Umbria 1996

Sometimes, by their actions, a person can bring down on their heads the very disaster they hope to avoid. Only now was Carlo beginning to see it. If only he'd been more tolerant, more understanding of a teenager's needs, his sister might have been a little more worldly, less inclined to seize freedom with both hands and not be so gullible, so easy for that circus boy to deceive. She wouldn't have felt the need to rebel against his own well-meaning discipline and advice. He should have taken her into his confidence earlier, explaining his plans for her future. When the time was right, he would have chosen the right husband for her and her life would have turned out quite differently. He wouldn't be facing the fallout of the bad situation in which she found herself now.

Less than two years after she had departed with her irresponsible lover, laughing hysterically as the man raised his fist in a mocking and obscene gesture as they drove away, his sister had returned home, shamed and defeated. He could still recall the sight of that garishly decorated circus vehicle as it disappeared into the dust on the road and his own feeling of helplessness at being unable to save the girl from herself. Even then he had known that this adventure was not going to end well.

Scarcely past her nineteenth birthday, Josefina looked careworn and years older now, her hair matted, her clothes faded and stiff with the mud and dust of the road. Nothing was left of the carefree teenager who had been such a delightful, innocent child. Almost home again, she was approaching the farmhouse slowly, unsure of her welcome and limping like an old woman, her feet bleeding through cracks in a pair of ill-fitting, broken-down shoes. Guarding a pregnancy, cradling her swollen belly in her arms, she was still minus a wedding ring. All this Carlo was able to take in at a glance. Although his heart went out to her, he was still a man of few words, an inarticulate farmer. In any case, he didn't know what to say.

'Yes, Carlo, it *is* me.' She stood at the back door, scarcely able to whisper through cracked lips. 'But I wouldn't blame you if you sent me on my way. I can't hide what's happened to me and I'll understand if you'd rather I didn't come home.'

Scarcely able to believe it was really Josefina, the little sister who had been so fastidious, sometimes showering more than once a day, Carlo stared at her for a full minute before relenting and sweeping her into his embrace.

'Oh, my darling girl,' he said. 'Of course you'll come in. This will always be your home.' In spite of the weight of her pregnancy, the girl felt thin and fragile in his arms.

And now, seated at the huge, well-worn table in the farmhouse kitchen, she was nursing a glass of water that Mancia, his wife, had grudgingly provided. Aware of the tension that had always existed between them, even before his sister went away, he was hoping that Mancia would leave them alone to talk. He knew Josefina would find it hard to speak freely under his wife's critical gaze. But instead, Mancia retreated to take up her customary position, leaning against the old-fashioned range, arms folded and scowling at her sister-in-law with no compassion in her gaze. Glancing at his wife, Carlo sighed, thinking she seemed even more grim and hatchet-faced than usual, her thin, black hair pulled into a bun and her thin lips folding inwards until they almost disappeared.

'Look at the state of her, Carlo.' Mancia pulled a face, holding a handkerchief to her

17

nose. 'She comes to you, reeking like a homeless person, pregnant and disgraced. We can't possibly let her come home now. What will the neighbours say?'

'Who cares what they have to say?' Carlo turned on her. 'Let he who is without sin cast the first stone.'

'Don't you dare quote scripture to me, Carlo Mancini. A heathen who hasn't been near a church in years. And, speaking of the Church, I'm sure the priest will have something to say about — ' And she rolled her eyes meaningfully towards the girl's obvious pregnancy.

'Ah, to hell with the — '

'Stop it, Carlo. You'll damn your immortal soul.'

'Cease your rattling, woman!' Angered at last, Carlo held up his hand for silence. 'I need to think.'

'What about? Supposing the circus people change their minds and come back for her? We could be robbed and murdered in our beds.'

'Don't be ridiculous.' Carlo's patience was coming to an end. 'Have you no pity, woman? Can't you see the poor girl's at the end of her tether?'

'Well, she has no one to blame but herself, if she is.'

'Carlo, I'll go.' Josefina put a hand to her back, rising awkwardly to her feet. 'I don't want to be the cause of trouble between you and your wife.'

'This is a fine time to think about trouble.' Mancia turned on her. 'A pity you didn't think of it before you spread your legs for that boy. Or was he not the only one?'

'Stop it, Mancia!' Carlo interrupted her before she could launch into another tirade. 'Of course Josefina will stay — she is my sister and this farm will always be her home. She wouldn't have come here if she had anywhere else to go.'

Josefina nodded, undone by her brother's kindness, biting her lips and squeezing her eyes shut to hold back the tears. All the same, one fat drop trickled down her cheek.

'Ssh!' Carlo moved to sit next to her, taking her small, grimy hand in his own huge one and placing it against his heart. 'You're safe now and everything's going to be all right. You'll see.'

Carlo's farm meant the whole world to him and he could already see an advantage in his sister's return. He spoke softly but his wife leaned forward, determined to catch his words.

'And when the baby is born and you feel more like yourself, you can help me once again with the horses.'

'And who's supposed to look after the child while she does? Me, I suppose? As if I haven't enough to do already.' Mancia was pink with indignation. 'But that's all you really care about, isn't it? Your stables and your wonderful horses.'

He turned to look at her then. 'Our horses provide your comfortable lifestyle, Mancia. Never forget that.'

'And don't you forget that my market stall with my vegetables and chickens keeps us going in the lean times. And there have been plenty of those lately.' Mancia stared around the shabby room with a sneer. 'I need to see to the fowls. They'll stop laying if I don't feed them and then where shall we be? Especially with two extra mouths to feed.' So saying, she snatched up the bucket of grain by the kitchen door and went out, slamming it hard enough to make the windows rattle.

'Don't worry. Her bark is much worse than her bite. She'll come around,' Carlo said when he was quite sure she had gone. Josefina smiled weakly, unable to be so sure.

With his wife out of the way, Carlo quickly cut some slices of her crusty, home-made bread and spread them with home-churned butter and cheese. His sister fell on them at once, obviously starving. No longer as fussy as she used to be, she ate quickly without troubling to wash her hands.

Carlo sighed, glancing at the rounded lump of her pregnancy. 'So when is the baby due?'

'I'm really not sure,' Josefina said when her mouth was no longer full and nodding assent as her brother held up the pot, offering coffee. 'It was a surprise to both of us. Drago was far from pleased.'

'And he still isn't going to marry you? Not even now?'

'No.' Josefina looked down at her hands, suddenly ill at ease. 'He has another girl already. Even younger than I am. She has a way of tossing her hair and giggling, shaking her breasts. Drago can't take his eyes off her.' Her voice dropped to a whisper. 'And he told me she knew things and could please him in a lot more ways than I ever did.'

'Oh, Josefina — '

'Don't say it. I was a fool all along and I know it. But he was so handsome, so attentive at first and he seemed so exotic, so exciting to me. He showed me their vehicles, painted with prancing horses and told me his father owned the circus and one day in the future, everything would be his. He spoke of the freedom of being out on the road and promised to make me a star of the circus. And I believed him, Carlo, because I wanted to. But it was all lies. His father was the ringmaster in charge of everything and only his stepsisters were allowed to perform in the ring. I was there just to groom and muck out the horses.'

'So why didn't you leave and come home?'

'Because I believed he was the love of my life and that he'd take care of me. But Drago won't take care of anyone — not even this new girl. We are all just toys to amuse him before we get broken and cast aside. He was so angry when he heard I was pregnant — said I'd done it on purpose to trap him. He wanted me to kill our child. The only person on my side was his mother, Loma. We had a lot in common because his sisters hated her for being their father's second wife. She knew how much I loved Drago and she kept hoping he'd do the right thing and marry me but I always knew he wouldn't.' She sighed, with all her weariness in it. 'And one day his mother got sick. A stroke, I think. She was lying in bed in her trailer, unable to move or speak. But Drago and his father were heartless. Cursing the inconvenience, they paused only to dump her in the emergency room of a hospital. They propped her up in a chair and the people there were so busy that nobody noticed at first. I wanted to stay with her to see what the doctors said and if they could help her but Drago and his father wouldn't wait. I couldn't believe the poor woman's husband and son could desert her, leaving her behind to be cared for by strangers or tossed aside to fend for herself. But that's what they did.'

'Oh, Josefina. You should have left there and then and come home.'

'How could I? I knew Mancia was glad to see the back of me. And I tried for so long to convince myself that Drago would have a change of heart. The last night we were together he was so kind and loving — like when we first met. Better still, he was accepting the idea of having the baby, or so I thought. He even made tea for me and watched me drink it. Then he lay with his arms around me until I went to sleep by the camp fire. I was happy that night for the first time in ages.' She sighed yet again. 'But of course it was just a trick. The tea was drugged and when I woke up, Drago, his father and the whole of the circus road train had already gone. I had been left all alone with only the clothes I was wearing, shivering by the dying embers of the fire. I had no money — no means of transport. I wasn't even sure where I was.'

'Well, you're home for good now, Josephina. Wipe your memory clear of those people and that treacherous young man. And in due time maybe you'll give me a healthy nephew to inherit the farm.'

'You want a child of mine to inherit the farm?' Josefina spoke softly as if she expected Mancia to come back and rage at her. 'So you don't think your wife will provide one?'

He laughed shortly. 'No. Not after ten years of marriage and still no sign of a child.' He thought for a moment and shrugged. 'She spends so long on her knees at bedtime, counting her beads in front of her shrine, I'm usually fast asleep by the time she joins me in bed. I think she does it on purpose, knowing I'm too tired to wait.'

'Oh, Carlo.'

'No, don't feel sorry for me. I knew what she was when I married her. A woman that devout should have taken the veil. It would have saved a lot of heartache and disappointment all round.' He held out his hand to help his sister to her feet and she clung to it, awkward and heavy in her pregnancy. 'But now you'll need a wash and then a good night's sleep. Your old room remains as you left it. Mancia wanted to change it and take in a lodger but who wants to lodge on a farm in the middle of nowhere? I wouldn't let her touch anything. Not even your clothes.'

Josefina shook her head. 'They won't fit me

now, even if they're still there.'

'I'll buy you some new ones then.' Not caring that she smelled of sweat and the grime of the road, he hugged her once more, kissing her cheek.

'Mancia won't like that.'

'Then Mancia can take a running jump.' He smiled widely for the first time. 'I've missed you so much, little sis. It's good to have you back home.'

★　★　★

Although he did his best not to show it when Josefina's baby arrived, Carlo couldn't hide his disappointment that the child was female and not the male heir he had been hoping for. Mancia smirked, pleased to see her husband's plans for the future thwarted. If she herself couldn't give him a son, she didn't want a nephew to replace him.

All the same, she argued with Josefina about her choice of name for the child.

'Aside from Loma, Rosalie was the only woman who was kind to me at the circus,' Josefina tried to explain. 'Many a time she dried my tears, trying to cheer me. She had very dark skin and hair — I think she was half Romany. She used to read tarot cards and it was amazing the things she knew. One day her people came for her and she left without saying goodbye. I want my little girl to carry that name in her memory.'

'Naming your child for a gypsy woman sounds unlucky to me.' Mancia sniffed. 'You would do better to name her for one of the better known saints. Give her something to live up to. Rosalie, indeed.'

'Rosalie was more real to me than any saint,' Josefina said, still feeling emotional after the birth. 'And she was beautiful. Maybe my child will be beautiful, too.'

'Too much beauty can be a curse.' Mancia sniffed again, peering at the little red scrap of humanity in Josefina's arms. 'Hasn't she enough to contend with already? A bastard whose father won't even acknowledge her?'

'Stop it, Mancia. That's quite enough.' Carlo put an end to his wife's tirade. 'This is Josie's child and if Rosalie is the name she has chosen, it's none of your business, or mine.'

'It is my business when I have to face the shame of a fallen woman living here in my home.' Mancia tossed her head, unwilling to be so easily defeated.

'Fallen woman? You should hear yourself. Nobody talks like that these days. And you might as well button your lip,' Carlo went on to say. 'This was my sister's home long before it became yours. She and her child will always be welcome here.'

'Oh, never mind me,' Mancia huffed like an angry chicken. 'Do as you please. You will, anyway.' So saying, she swept out of the kitchen, letting the door bang behind her.

★   ★   ★

Josefina's baby proved to be a healthy child who went from strength to strength, raised on the good, wholesome food provided by the farm. She was on horseback almost from the time she could walk and both she and her mother spent as much time as they could with the horses they loved. It was also a way of staying clear of Mancia who would otherwise find chores to keep them both occupied. They knew also that she was uneasy around the big animals who sensed her fear and enjoyed teasing her, crowding her and snorting in her face, making her squeal in fright.

But, with the horse racing industry in Italy in disarray and some tracks closing down altogether, Carlo had to keep ahead of the times by turning his attention to breeding and training heavier, sturdier animals that people might keep for the pleasure of riding or for hunting hares and wild pigs.

And when she grew older, in spite of Rosalie's protests, Josefina sent her to school, determined that she should receive at least the rudiments of an education. The girl didn't do well there, resenting the time she had to spend indoors away from the horses. She didn't make friends easily and knew the children whispered about her, sniggering behind their hands. Not because she was a bastard; more than one child had to live with that stigma. But the story of how her mother ran off with the circus people and her ignominious return was all too well known and recounted with relish. How that proud and fastidious sister of Carlo Mancini, rumoured to bathe twice a day and who thought herself too good for the local farm boys, had returned home in disgrace; dirty, unkempt, with an obvious pregnancy and no man willing to own it.

Rosalie put up with school until she was fourteen, when she played truant as often as she could and despised most of the other children as petty-minded and immature. She was truly happy only when she was working with horses, sometimes witnessing the miracle of bringing new foals into the world — which almost always happened at night — and later training them to a lead rein. Eager to learn, she watched everything

Uncle Carlo did and was quick to realize when a young animal was willing to let her ride. She had a ready excuse for the school if anyone asked after her; she would tell them her mother was sick and that she was needed at home. And, ultimately, when this proved to be true, she felt herself largely to blame for Josefina's illness. She had told the same lie too often and made it come true.

Her mother's decline was fast. By the time she admitted she was unwell and persuaded to visit a doctor, the cancer was too far advanced for anything but palliative care. It had spread to most of her internal organs and soon it was impossible for her to eat. She could sleep only as much as the pain permitted while she waited to die. Day and night Rosalie sat by her bedside, clutching her mother's hand and weeping.

'I'm so sorry, Mama. This is all my fault.'

'Oh Rosalie, don't.' Josefina couldn't speak above a whisper. 'You are the best daughter a woman could ever have. You have nothing to blame yourself for.'

'But I do. I do. You don't know the half of it.'

'Doesn't matter now.' She was getting breathless, finding it hard to speak. 'Take good care of your Uncle Carlo. He has no life with — that woman — she's no more than a nun without a veil.' And she tried to laugh silently until she lapsed into a fit of coughing while Rosalie tried to laugh with her and ended up crying instead. Only months after the onset of her illness, Josefina was dead.

The joy seemed to go out of Carlo's life now his sister was gone. He and Rosalie trained up a fine pair of greys that were sold to a racing stable in England; the last of his thoroughbreds. But even this success couldn't please him.

'Uncle, you have to stop grieving,' Rosalie told him. 'I miss her, too, more than anything and if I find something to laugh about, it still feels like a betrayal. But she wouldn't want that. She would want us to look forward to the future and get on with our lives.'

'Easier said than done.' Carlo shook his head. 'When she left with that circus boy, I thought I'd lost her forever and then she came back — only for me to lose her all over again. I'm a lot older than she was — I should have been first to go.'

'Things don't always turn out that way,' she said, anxious that her uncle shouldn't get maudlin and sentimental. 'And I think you need a distraction.' She spread out a newspaper in front of him, drawing his attention to a horse sale, advertised to take place during the following week. 'See? And it isn't so far to go. You're in funds right now from the sale of the greys. Let's go to this auction and buy a couple of mares before Mancia decides to give all your money away to the Church.'

'She would, too, if she knew where I kept it.' He looked at the advertisement and sighed. 'I don't know, Rosalie — maybe next time. My heart just isn't in it these days.'

'Well, mine is. Buy them for me and let me take care of them, then. If I'm idle, Mancia will make me clean out the chicken house or plant endless rows of vegetables. Worse, she might make me go back to school.'

'Good luck to her with that.' Carlo's smile was wry. 'I wouldn't try to make you do anything you don't want. Look at you — just as headstrong and wilful as your mother. And you look more and more like her as you get older.'

'We're good for next week, then?'

'I dunno, Rosalie. I'm worn out. I need to rest for a while.'

'You can rest when you're dead. I won't let you sit here and brood.'

Carlo sighed. 'You're even more of a bully than my wife. What did I do to deserve two such women in my life?'

'You don't have to do anything, Uncle Carlo. I'll make all the arrangements about the sale. I'll even drive us there.'

'You will not. I might let you drive a bit round the farm but you don't have a licence and you're still only fourteen years old!'

'Ha, ha! That made you sit up and think, didn't it?'

'You little minx.' Carlo made a grab for her but she danced away, out of reach.

Carlo wasn't lying when he said he was tired. He was also short of breath and that indigestive pain was back. He really should get some antacid pills. All the same, he gave in to Rosalie and took her to the sale that was to be held nearby. There, they were both so intent on getting a bargain, they didn't realize they had come to the attention of a swarthy, gypsy-looking man with longish black hair speckled with grey. Positioned on the opposite side of the ring, he was chain-smoking and watching the Mancinis through the smoke haze with narrowed eyes, inter-ested to see what they were buying.

'What is it, Drago?' his companion teased him, poking him in the ribs.

'Getting the hots for that little farm girl? Bit young for you, isn't she? Can't be more than fourteen. Scarcely old enough to grow a pair of tits.'

'Shut your dirty mouth,' Drago growled at him. 'You remember Josie, don't you?'

'Sure I do. Prettiest girl you ever had. Loyal, too. You ain't had a girl like that one since.'

'Yeah, well. Never know what you've got till you lose it. Josie came from some place hereabouts and that kid looks just like her. Taller than most and with the same tangled mess of red hair. She might even be my own daughter.'

'Garn. That's a bit of a stretch, isn't it?'

'She'd be about the right age. Do me a favour, Gino. Go over an' chat to them. Find out who they are. Where they live.'

'Nah. The old man'll think I'm after the girl.'

'So what? You can be likeable enough when you try. Go an' speak to them before they pay up and leave.'

'It'll cost yer, then.'

'Yeah an' it'll cost you a bloody nose if you don't get over there right away.'

'I won't know what to say,' Gino whined.

'That horse they just bought. Say your boss wanted it, missed it, an' he'd like to know if they'll sell it on now.'

'An' what if they say yes? You've spent all your money already.'

'They won't.' Drago waved his hand impatiently. 'Farmers don't waste a whole day buying horses to sell them on right away.' He gave Gino a shove. 'Get over there quick. Looks like they're getting ready to leave.'

Less than half an hour later Gino was back, smirking and pleased with himself.

'You're right. They won't sell their new horses. But they do have a smallholding back down the track where they breed and sell horses, mostly to farmers these days. The name's Mancini — '

'Yes!' Drago punched the air in glee. 'It is them. I was right. Thanks, Gino. I know where they live now.'

'Just a moment.' Gino looked puzzled. 'You couldn't wait to get rid of Josie and her baby all those years ago. What's so different now?'

'Everything. She's not a baby any more. All the hard work on her has already been done. An' I've been watching her. She might be young but she knows her way around horses. See how she advises the man when he leans in to listen to her.'

'Bollocks,' Gino exclaimed. 'He's probably deaf. You're just seeing what you want to see.'

'No. I see what she could become. A new act to liven things up and bring a bit of sparkle and glamour to the show. My sisters won't face it but they're getting too old for this game. People want to see youth and freshness — not painted old tarts waving stringy arms and trying to stand up on the back of a horse.'

'Phew! Better not let them hear you say that. They'll have your balls for a necklace. An' what makes you think that girl ain't happy enough where she is? Look at her — she's not hurtin' any. Why should she want to join a circus?'

Drago's smile was sly. 'Her mother did, didn't she?'

* * *

'I'd know you anywhere, girl,' Drago said, looking at Rosalie. He recognized the Mancini farm as soon as he saw it. And now he had the girl in his sights, he had no intention of wasting time discussing the merits of horses he was never going to buy. Instead he came straight to the point. 'You're Josefina's daughter.'

'Yes. I am. But how did you know?' Rosalie stared at him in amazement.

'And what's it to you if she is?' Carlo didn't like the way the conversation was going and placed himself squarely between them, suspicious of this smartly dressed traveller who had been watching them so intently at the horse sale and now seemed to be cosying up to his niece. He massaged his breast bone

35

and sighed, wishing he didn't feel so tired all the time — and that pain was coming back like a knife in his chest. 'I thought you were here to buy horses? Not chase after Rosalie. She may be tall for her age but she's still only fourteen years old . . . '

'Sorry — sorry.' Drago raised his hands in surrender. 'I should have said so at once — I'm not here to buy horses. An' I'm not interested in Rosalie — not in the way you think. I have every reason to believe she could be my daughter . . . '

Carlo leaned on the fence for support, his temper rising along with the shortness of breath. 'If that's so, you can get out of here now. You left my sister without any money — alone and destitute on the road. Only dogged determination brought her back to us. You let your child grow up a bastard and now you have the hide to barge in here, trying to claim her.' He had more to say but his anger and the pain in his chest was making him breathless. 'Go. Get off my land now.'

By now Mancia had heard the raised voices and, realizing there was an argument, came outside to see what was amiss.

'You don't understand,' Drago persisted. 'It's obvious that the girl knows her way around horses. Let me take her with me and I'll make her the star of our show. She'll be famous.' He was speaking to Carlo but watching Rosalie out of the corner of his eye. He could see he had her attention and sensed that she didn't share her uncle's sentiments.

'Just go!' Carlo was red in the face now and even more breathless.

'Carlo, wait. Why be so hasty? So rude,' Mancia said. She had been quick to take note of Drago's modern transport and respectable clothes. 'The man has taken the trouble to drive over here. This may be a great opportunity for Rosalie.' At long last she could see a chance to be rid of the child she had never wanted. 'You should at least hear what he has to offer.'

'The voice of reason at last.' Summoning all his charm, Drago turned to Mancia, ready to impress. He took her calloused hand in his own gloved one, bending over it to make an extravagant bow, ever the showman, through and through.

'Ohh!' Mancia was for once at a loss for words, unused to such courtesy.

'Just leave.' Carlo ground out the words. 'Now. Before I get my gun.'

'I get the message. Keep your hair on.' Drago wasn't in the least unnerved. Taking his time, he pressed a business card into Mancia's hand. 'I'll leave that with you, Signora.' This he accompanied with a saucy wink. 'We'll be in the area for another month or so. In case he changes his mind.' Deliberately, he was ignoring Rosalie, all too aware of her wide-eyed admiration. His little fish had taken the bait.

'I won't,' Carlo croaked, scarcely able to speak now.

No one said any more but all three of them watched as Drago sprang into his van and drove off with a cheery wave.

Rosalie watched until it was totally lost to view in a cloud of dust on the road. 'Do you think,' she said dreamily and to no one in particular, 'that beautiful man really is my father?'

She was distracted by a scream from Mancia. By now Carlo was lying on the ground, fighting for breath and his wife in a state of panic was on her knees beside him.

'Oh Rosalie, hurry,' she said, wringing her hands. 'Find a telephone and send for an ambulance. I think Carlo is having a heart attack.'

Rosalie ran as fast as she could and found Carlo's telephone. But by the time an ambulance was able to reach the farm, slowed by the uneven country road, Carlo was gone and could not be revived.

His funeral took place a week later. Spring was giving way to summer and the weather becoming hot, so there was no reason for any delay. Mancia was well-known locally because of her market stall, if not as well-liked as her husband, so people from the surrounding area as well as from neighbouring farms were keen to come to his funeral. Mancia and Rosalie sat together in the front row, having little to say to each other. Later, Mancia told anyone who would listen that she thought Rosalie largely to blame for her husband's death.

'What am I to do now?' The woman had spent the whole of the previous week in tears although Rosalie suspected her lamentations were all for herself. 'A widow woman alone with a farm to look after? And what about bills and taxes — all that paperwork? Your uncle always took care of that.'

'I don't know, Aunt.' Rosalie sighed. She missed her uncle terribly and was growing tired of Mancia's self-pity and endless complaints.

'Oh, you're hard.' Mancia sniffled. 'I haven't seen you shed one tear for him yet.'

'Shut up,' Rosalie finally lost it and yelled. 'Just shut up! I loved Uncle Carlo — much more than you ever did. All you care about is your stupid church.'

She ran into her bedroom and placed a chair under the handle although she thought it unlikely that Mancia would follow her there. Why oh why had she persuaded her uncle to buy more horses? Now she would have to train and sell them before she could leave. There was no way she could stay with her uncle gone; no way to live with Mancia from whom she had never received a kind word. Later, exhausted, she slept although she woke up early, thinking of the needs of the horses. There was no one else to tend them now.

She reached the stables in time to see a horse float backing up to the stable doors. Ignoring her, the driver jumped down from the cab and opened the back of his truck, setting down a ramp.

'Morning!' She hurried over. 'I think you've made a mistake. We've no horses for sale here today.'

'Not what Signora Mancini told me.' The driver pushed past, ignoring her. 'An' I've got the cash for the nags in my pocket, so stand aside. I'm taking these nags off your hands today.'

'Nags? These are not nags — they're good quality hunters. Oh please, wait a moment. I'm sure there has been some mistake.'

'No mistake, Rosalie.' Mancia had arrived, breathless as she had run from the house. 'Go on. Take them.' She made a shooing gesture at the man who was now hovering, uncertain. 'Take them all.'

'No, not my little Shetland! Not Beppo, too?' Rosalie was aghast.

'Why not? You've no use for him, have you? Carlo said you'd outgrown him years ago,' Mancia snapped.

'I know that. But he was old when he came to us — the companion of a skittish racehorse. And anyway you can't sell him — he's my pet.' For the first time since her uncle's death, Rosalie felt close to tears. It seemed as if her whole world was falling apart.

'Tears now, is it?' Mancia sneered. 'No tears for my poor Carlo but tears for the loss of a pony on the way to the knackers' yard.'

'What did you say?' Rosalie turned on her. 'You are selling these lovely animals to someone for horsemeat?'

'Why not? I can't be doing with horses. They're of no use to me.' Mancia shrugged. 'I'll rub along well enough with my market stall and the chickens. Horses? No.'

'Please, Mancia, I've never asked you for anything in the whole of my life. Don't do this, please. I'll get down on my knees in the mud and beg if I have to.'

'Don't be so stupid. I can't afford to feed

pets. There's no room for sentiment on a farm.'

'That circus man. He came looking for horses. He'll buy them and treat them well — even my pony.' Tears were pouring down Rosalie's face now, blinding her so that she couldn't see Mancia's self-satisfied smile. 'He said he thought he might be my father — and if he's kind, he'll do it for me. He gave you his card, didn't he — if you still have it?'

Ignoring Rosalie, Mancia turned to speak to the van driver who had lit a cigarette and was leaning against the side of his truck and smoking, waiting to see what would happen. 'I'm sorry you've had a wasted journey, my man.' She fished in her pocket and offered him a small wad of money which he checked and stuffed into the top pocket of his shirt. 'We're done. I'll be in touch if I need you again.'

Rosalie never thought to question why Drago, driving a horse box and accompanied by Gino, should have arrived so promptly less than an hour later. Happy to accept her father's invitation to leave with him, she packed her possessions and those of her mother, which were surprisingly few, and left her uncle's farm without a backward glance. Relieved as she was to have saved their horses from an untimely end and escaped the drudgery and boredom of life with Mancia, she didn't think to consider if joining an itinerant circus troupe on the road was really what she wanted to do.

2

It didn't take long for Rosalie to realize she had made a terrible mistake; that she had been cleverly manipulated by Mancia in collusion with Drago. To begin with, she wasn't certain Drago really was her biological father but she wanted so desperately to get away from Mancia that she didn't care. Later, as time went by, more and more of their similarities came to light. Although he was dark as she was fair like her mother, they had the same dark eyes — that in Rosalie's case were quite startling against a background of reddish-gold hair and they had the same mannerism of holding their heads on one side when they were considering something. They even had the same way of pursing their lips when annoyed.

She was also beginning to understand the downside of constantly moving from place to place and belonging nowhere. People were happy enough to see them arrive and be entertained by the show but no one expected them to stay. The lifestyle that had seemed so appealing from the outside was no more than smoke and mirrors — a tinsel glamour that didn't entirely hide the grime and dust of the road. Although she had lived simply on her uncle's farm with few modern facilities, she was beginning to appreciate the clean, fresh-tasting water that came via a mountain spring and Mancia's plentiful supply of eggs and vegetables that meant they would never go hungry. On the road she was famished a lot of the time because there was never enough to eat. Nobody seemed to care if she went to bed half-starved and with her stomach growling, keeping her awake.

But when she had been faced with the threat of that man from the abattoir in his filthy truck, ready to whisk their horses away to an untimely death, she was given little time to consider her options. She could see no alternative other than joining the circus to save them. Drago had been a good storyteller too, painting a romantic picture of a carefree life on the road that proved to be very different from the reality. And having insulted Mancia by being so ready to leave, Rosalie knew there could be no turning back. She had been quick to realize that life on the farm without Carlo and the horses would be very different; she would be nothing but an unpaid servant to Mancia who had a strong work ethic and didn't believe that a teenager needed to have any fun.

But now she was beginning to understand how much she had taken Mancia's house-keeping skills for granted. These travellers gave little consideration to hygiene or cleanliness, and would usually leave a site decorated with filth and rubbish whenever they had to move on. It didn't endear them to the local populace and it was easy to see why they wouldn't be welcome to return. And, far from being a cheerful, happy-go-lucky band of showmen, the circus camp was far from happy. Most performers felt exploited and cheated by Drago who paid them as little as possible, thinking they should be grateful to work in a circus at all. As a consequence, they were surly and humourless away from the ring. Having stayed on after the death of The Great Ernesto, Drago's father, they had hoped his son would breathe new life into the enterprise, only to be disappointed yet again. Their best trapeze artiste had been head-hunted by a much larger troupe and had already left. Morale was at an all-time low.

Up early one morning, she came upon him making a deal with two men over the two horses from her uncle's farm and he was stuffing a wad of money into his coat as he watched the animals being led away.

'Papa!' she called out before she could stop

herself. 'What are you doing? Where are those horses going?'

Drago shrugged and raised an eyebrow before answering her. 'To a better life, I hope. They're thoroughbreds — too valuable for us to keep here.'

'That's not what you said when you bought them from Mancia for next to nothing. You said they were nags.'

'Whatever. It's no business of yours, anyway.' Irritated by her questions, he turned his back.

'And Beppo? I hope you didn't sell him, too?'

'Too old,' he said, shrugging dismissively. 'He'll have to earn his keep here as best he may. Edmond is in the ring with him now, trying to train him. I don't have great hopes.'

Rosalie didn't wait to hear more but ran towards the big tent, hoping that Edmond, whoever he was, would be kind and patient with her old friend. She recognized some of the clowns out of costume indulging in wrestling and horseplay on the edge of the ring but the noise didn't seem to disturb Beppo, who was carrying a tiny man on his back as he went over a series of small jumps. She was surprised to see that Edmond wasn't a young person like herself or even one of the clowns. He was a dwarf.

As soon as he saw her, Beppo forgot all his instructions and cantered across the ring to see her. She greeted him, burying her face in his neck and breathing in the familiar horsy scent of his golden mane. Only after a moment did she look up and speak to his rider.

'I'm sorry,' she said. 'I'm interrupting your work.'

'No matter,' the man smiled at her, lighting up a face so beautiful it was almost angelic, framed with a halo of golden curls. 'We're almost done for today. You're Drago's daughter, aren't you? He told me Beppo used to be yours.'

'Yes,' she said. 'Until I outgrew him.' She put a hand over her mouth. 'Oh, I'm sorry — I didn't mean — '

'It's OK.' The little man smiled at her. 'I've learned not to be sensitive about my stature.' His voice was deep and melodious, not at all the childish squeak she had expected. He was probably about the same age as her father but his eyes were full of kindness and compassion, very different from Drago's calculating gaze.

'Come with me,' he said. 'I'm going to give Beppo a rub-down and some hay now — he deserves a treat after his work-out. I'm sure he'd like you to spend some time with him.'

Rosalie nodded, happy to have made a friend in the troupe at last. Unable to forget that she was Drago's daughter, most of the girls were wary of befriending her. Edmond, she soon discovered, was a law unto himself. She found him an easy, undemanding companion and she spent the rest of the afternoon with him when he invited her into his trailer to have some tea. He kept his trailer as clean and neat as his person, although he had not been expecting a visitor. Neither of them mentioned it but, although she remained there for the whole afternoon, no one came in search of her or seemed to care where she was.

Edmond told her something of his life on the road with the circus and even that once he had a wife but she knew he was leaving an awful lot out. There was an air of sadness about him and sorrow behind his expressive grey eyes but she knew it was too early in their friendship for him to tell her his secrets, if he ever would. But, from that day onward, she spent as much time as possible with Edmond and Beppo. They were the only ones who made life bearable here.

Although he spoke Italian like a native, Edmond was English and he found a willing pupil in Rosalie who was keen to learn as much as she could of that language.

'One day I want to go to America,' she told her new friend. 'See Disneyland.'

'There's a lot more to America than Disneyland,' Edmond started to say.

'I don't care,' Rosalie said. 'That's where I want to go first. You'll probably have to take me yourself because my father won't.'

Edmond frowned slightly, biting his lip, sad to hear she was so disillusioned with Drago already.

When she left the farm for the last time, she'd had such high hopes for the future. Now she was finding it hard to believe there was such a huge gap between her expectations and the actual experience of life on the road. Drago had let her believe he cared for her and that she would figure largely in his life but the reality was very different. The idea of having a daughter must have tickled his vanity for a while but the novelty soon wore off and he returned to his usual pattern of chasing women, impatient of any intrusion from Rosalie.

Already a dashing figure in his red tailcoat, jodhpurs, shiny black boots, pristine white shirt and top hat, he could turn the head of any girl. Promoting himself as the colourful circus owner, he picked them up on his travels and just as quickly discarded them, sometimes leaving them without any money to get back home. Rosalie soon realized this must be how he had treated her mother. No wonder Josefina never cared to speak of her days on the road. Drago's fancy manners and good looks were no more than a sham, hiding a selfish, even brutal personality.

Worse, she found out he had lied to her repeatedly about her role in the show and what it was likely to be. He let her believe his stepsisters were a couple of kindly older women who would welcome her with open arms, happy to teach her their skills. He told her they were tired of performing and would be more than willing to take a well-earned rest. Once again, this wasn't the case.

Cleo and Cassia were tiny in stature; a pair of gimlet-eyed, sharp-featured pixie women, close in age and similar enough to be taken for twins. They saw Rosalie as a threat to their position as stars of the ring and united in spite against her. They made her feed, groom and do all the chores for their horses while they sat outside their trailer with their feet up, smoking and drinking gin.

This continued until Rosalie felt brave enough to tackle them and ask when her own training was likely to begin. The sisters exchanged meaningful glances and laughed in her face.

'You!' Cleo stood up and poked her in the

chest with a pointed red fingernail. 'Just because you're Drago's daughter, you think you're better than us.'

'I don't. Really, I — '

'Save your words for someone who cares. I hear you're spending a lot of time with Edmond. You do know he has a bit of a reputation, don't you?' She gave a knowing smirk. 'You want to be careful there. He isn't small all over, you know.'

Rosalie felt herself blushing. She knew exactly what Cleo meant but she didn't know why she should be the target of so much malice. It left her temporarily at a loss for words.

Encouraged by her silence, Cleo kept going. 'Cat got your tongue? No wonder. A farm girl with no personality and little talent, that I can see.'

'Come on, Cleo, that isn't fair,' Cassia chimed in, seeing Rosalie's stricken expression. 'She doesn't know how to answer you. She's just a kid.'

But encouraged by Rosalie's silence, Cleo wasn't ready to let it go. She continued on the attack. 'What makes you think you've got what it takes? What do you know of showmanship? Of captivating an audience? And as for taking over the bare-backed riding from us — ' To emphasize her point, she hawked and spat a gob of phlegm, narrowly missing Rosalie's boots and making her flinch. 'That day is a long way off. We were trained in Paris by a woman who performed before most of the crowned heads of Europe — '

'Then that was a long time ago.' Rosalie's temper rose along with her courage and she found herself also capable of spite. 'There aren't too many of those left.'

'Don't interrupt.' Cleo's cheeks reddened at this slur on her age. 'We've enough to do keeping fit ourselves without wasting our time on a lost cause like you. If Drago wants you to have some sort of role in the circus, he'd better train you himself.'

'And good luck with that,' Cassia added with a wry smile. 'Our little brother isn't the most patient of men.'

For the first time since she had joined the circus, someone had told Rosalie the truth. But she reminded herself that she was a good rider and, after all, how difficult was it going to be? She had only to keep her balance and stand upright on the back of a horse. And the circus horses were used to it, weren't they? They probably went no faster than a gentle canter.

But it wasn't like that at all. Resenting his sisters' refusal to help her, Drago took out his frustration on Rosalie. The truth was that although he was the owner and ringmaster now his father was gone, he had never been much of a performer himself. He had no head for heights so he couldn't work on the trapeze. He had learned only to handle a stockman's whip, taught by an itinerant cowboy from Australia who had joined the circus for the summer season a few years ago. Knowing that one day he would be ringmaster, he had honed this one skill until he could lasso and capture an animal on the run or flick the tip of the whip to pluck a single leaf from a twig. But he wasn't a rider and hadn't the first idea how to teach a girl to balance and stand up on the back of a horse. His stepsisters were well aware of this, of course.

And, far from being gentle, well-trained ponies, the horses of Faustino's Travelling Circus were unusually frisky and seemed to have minds of their own. Rosalie suspected they had been specially chosen for her; Cleo was sure to know which ones would cause the most trouble. Luckily, due to the erratic behaviour of the first horse she was given, she suspected and found a burr under his saddle. She didn't want to accuse anyone — they were sure to deny it — so she removed it quickly and never mentioned it to her father.

All the same, she reminded herself to be vigilant around Cleo.

Her first session under Drago's tuition didn't go well. She managed to stay on for a moment or so without falling off but he wasn't impressed.

'Idiot girl! I thought you said you could ride. You're supposed to make it look elegant — effortless! Instead, you put me in mind of a bent monkey on a stick.'

'Give me a chance, Papa. I will try harder. After all, this is only my first day.'

'And don't call me Papa in front of the others. Remember — in the ring I am always Signor Faustino or sir.'

'All right — sir,' she said in a small voice.

'We'll try again tomorrow but I can't see you replacing Cleo or Cassia any time soon.' Impatiently, he was tapping a whip on the side of his boot. He always carried a whip of some kind, encouraging people to think he could ride. 'In the meantime, you can keep on grooming and mucking out horses. At least you can make yourself useful there.'

Rosalie, feeling utterly miserable, felt imminent tears stinging her eyes. She had hoped for at least one word of encouragement but Drago merely raised an eyebrow and shrugged. 'Well? What are you waiting for? We're done here for today. You can go.'

Blinded by tears and disappointed in this man of whom she had expected so much, Rosalie fled, meaning to go to the trailer she shared with the youngest trapeze girl and have a good, self-pitying weep. She wanted to get there before Cleo or Cassia saw her and taunted her yet again.

'Hey, hey, Rosalie, what's up?' Edmond caught up with her. 'Dry those tears and don't let your old man see he's upset you — he'll only do it again.'

'I know.' Rosalie tried to smile through her tears and failed.

'Come on — I'll make you some tea and you'll tell me all about it. A trouble shared, eh?' he said, putting an arm round her waist although he could scarcely reach it and steering her up the steps to his newly painted trailer.

'I don't want to put you to any bother,' she whispered.

'Nonsense. We're friends, aren't we? Friends look out for each other. You don't need to tell me anything about that old man of yours. A selfish, sadistic bastard through and through, like his father before him.'

'You shouldn't let him hear you say that. He said I was disrespectful just for calling him Papa.'

The dwarf snorted. 'I know how to handle

Drago. And that stockman's whip he's so proud of. I'm a lot stronger than I look.'

Rosalie looked at him, unsure he could live up to these brave words.

Over a warming cup of tea, she poured out all her heartbreak and disappointment while Edmond encouraged her to hold nothing back. Only when she had come to the end of her tale, did he speak.

'I'm afraid Drago has an unrealistic vision of the future for this little outfit. It has never been more than a small, traditional family circus at best but he's always had big ideas and there's no one to put the brakes on him now. He wants to copy that big French circus — you know the one — ' He clicked his fingers, searching for the name. 'He dreams of hiring top acts to draw in the crowds. But he has no real capital so how can he hope to compete? He's already spent what money he had on a much bigger tent to house an impressive trapeze. Rumour has it that he wants the artistes to perform without a safety net to give the audience even greater thrills. This is why the last guy left in a hurry. Drago said he was head-hunted but that isn't so. The guy wasn't willing to take such risks — not for himself or for the girls he must catch.'

Rosalie stared at him in horror, waiting for Edmond to continue with his tale.

'Drago won't see that it's the traditional, old-fashioned circus that people like. The nostalgia. The simple things, like Punch and Judy. Some years ago, before television made the world small, most circuses had wild animals — it was the only way for people to see them, apart from the zoo. But Ernesto realized those days were done and gradually phased them out. In any case, there was too much aggravation from do-gooders and animal rights protesters. Now we have ponies and performing dogs and that's as it should be. We don't need so-called lion-tamers or old-fashioned thrills and spills. Just happy, harmless entertainment for the amusement of children.' He sighed, shaking his head. 'But when Drago took over, he sacked all the old clowns — the gentle ones that the children loved. You've seen the clowns we have now. Aside from Luca, who believes in the old ways like me, they're just raucous young men who shout and throw things at each other, including buckets of water. They frighten the children in the front rows, making them cry. One family had such a soaking, they had to get up and leave.'

'Oh, no.'

'And I'm not telling you this to upset you, Rosalie, but to warn you before you get in too deep. With Drago in charge, this outfit is surely doomed. Young as you are, if you can, you should leave here right now. Go back to where you came from before it's too late.'

Rosalie shook her head. 'It's already too late.' And she told Edmond how she had been tricked into leaving with Drago and joining the circus. 'My uncle's wife never liked me — she wouldn't have me back again — ever.'

'I see.'

'Do you? I wish I did. I don't know what will happen now. Drago's disappointed in me and I'm sure he regrets taking me away from the farm. I saw him selling the horses he had from my aunt — he'd sell me as well, if he could.'

'Now, Rosalie!'

'Well, he would. And Beppo, too, except he's too old.'

'Ah, Beppo.' Edmond frowned, biting his lip.

'What about him?' Rosalie's heart lurched at the thought of something happening to her brave little horse. 'Go on, you might as well tell me the worst.'

'Let's just say he has different plans for Beppo. And me.' Edmond looked away, unwilling to say any more.

'Edmond, you're frightening me. What plans?'

Edmond puffed his cheeks in a long sigh.

'Drago has always loved tricks with fire. He made a couple of clowns learn to juggle with flaming torches. Now he wants me to train Beppo to jump through a ring of fire.'

'No! You can't let him do that. There was a fire in our stables once and Beppo was terrified.'

Edmond scratched his head. 'I'll mention it but I doubt if Drago will change his mind.'

'Edmond, I hate to say this because you're the only friend I have. But you should leave here yourself — right now while you still can.'

'Oh? Like you, I have nowhere to go. There aren't many options for people like me, you know.'

'What about films? You're a good actor, I've seen you, and you have a wonderful voice. There has to be a demand for little people like you. Your face is quite beautiful, too.'

'That's part of the problem, my sweet. They want people like me to be ugly so we can play goblins and gnomes.'

'But surely — '

'Don't think I haven't already tried. The only work I was offered aside from this was to work in corporate entertainment.'

'Corporate entertainment? That doesn't sound so bad.'

'You think? I don't suppose you've ever

seen a party of drunken salesmen at a conference, entertaining themselves by making fun of a little man?'

'No, I haven't.'

'I did try that line of work for a while. And at first it wasn't so bad. To begin with there was just a bit of harmless teasing but after a while the mood changed and things began to get physical. I had a friend thrown into a swimming pool with all his clothes on, including his shoes; they thought it was funny when he almost drowned. Then at another party, some of the men were too drunk to know what they were doing; they tossed one of us across the room, calling for someone to catch him. Then they started treating him like a football. Eventually, the guy was dropped, broke his back and has been in a wheelchair ever since.'

Appalled, Rosalie could only stare at him in horror.

Edmond laughed shortly. 'So now you can see why Faustino's Travelling Circus doesn't seem so bad, after all.'

3

Under Edmond's patient tuition, Beppo learned first to jump through the empty hoops with the little man on his back and, although Drago kept urging him to move on to the next stage, he insisted on taking his time over setting fire to the hoops. If the little Shetland were to take fright and lose confidence now, it would take some time to regain it. Drago could do nothing but grind his teeth and wait as Edmond refused to give him a time frame. A lot of the time Rosalie sat close at hand, watching them; she knew her presence was a comfort to Beppo, encouraging him to try harder.

To Rosalie's relief, her father had given up on her own 'training' at least for the time being. She resolved to try working on a new act alone, away from his critical gaze. In the hope of discovering their secrets and copying their technique, she spied on the sisters at rehearsal, watching them from behind a curtain. Unfortunately, they seemed to possess a sixth sense that told them when she was there, so they stuck to their old routines and never let her see anything out of the ordinary.

She understood now that she had exchanged one life of drudgery for another and knew she couldn't live like this forever as the general gofer and maid of all work around the circus. If there was any messy or tedious job to be done, Rosalie was expected to do it. So far as she was concerned, the only good thing to come out of her banishment from the ring was that Drago ceased to show any interest in her and seemed happy to leave her alone.

So she was surprised when one of the clowns faced up to him, taking her part and insisting that since she was doing the work, she deserved to be properly paid. Luca had already negotiated better wages for himself and the other clowns. Tall as Drago and with a loping stride and lazy smile, he put Rosalie in mind of an old-fashioned cowhand; he even wore Western clothes, except when he was dressed for the ring in white make-up, oversized shoes and baggy pants. Not wanting to hear what he had to say, Drago blustered at first, trying to dismiss his request.

'Why? Why should I pay her? The girl is my daughter and still only fourteen years old.'

'Fifteen,' Rosalie said. 'I had a birthday last week.'

The clown stared Drago down, not to be

put off. 'The lass works as hard as any man — I've seen her,' he said. 'And you know the saying. 'The labourer is worthy of his hire.' Pay the girl from the time she joined us, or I'll stir up trouble with the unions.'

'Ah, the unions!' Drago scoffed. 'D'you think they give a damn about people like you? Transients who move around all the time?'

'I'll make it my business to see that they do. There's also the question of exploiting a young person, too.' The clown was calm but determined — a burly, formidable figure without his red wig and crazy clothes.

Drago won the argument by refusing to pay the full amount. All the same, Rosalie had more money than she'd ever seen in the whole of her life and didn't know what to do with it. Finally, she decided to sew it into her mattress but she waited to do this until the girl sharing her trailer had gone to her practice session on the trapeze. The girl despised anyone who didn't work the trapeze, including Rosalie, so they had never become real friends.

★　★　★

The circus was drawing closer and closer to Rome and Rosalie was excited at the prospect of seeing the city. They were to perform for a week in a small town on the outskirts where Drago had been engaged in promotion and trying to drum up new sponsors. Now he decided it was time to try out the new acts, including Beppo the Fearless Wonder Horse, Who Can Leap Through the Rings of Fire. Edmond had pleaded for just one ring to begin with but Drago insisted on three 'to make a proper show'.

In addition, the new big top could house a larger trapeze although, without exception, the artistes refused to go up without a safety net underneath.

'No net — no performance,' they insisted, forcing Drago to concede to their wishes. This put him in a bad mood. So far as he was concerned, nothing was going according to plan. But finally it was time for the real show. A Saturday night and the tickets all sold, miraculously changing Drago's mood. He hid his thoughts well but he smiled a lot, showing his newly polished, gleaming white teeth.

The first half of the show proceeded as planned with the clowns making the audience laugh at their rough play, and then Cleo and Cassia showed their effortless expertise, even leaping from horse to horse as the crowd cheered. They were still a very popular act and there were sweets and flowers thrown into the ring as the sisters departed, blowing kisses to everyone as they went.

The trapeze artistes came on next, once the safety net had been erected.

'What a waste of time,' Drago grumbled. 'See how it slows everything down?'

'Better safe than sorry. And it gives the crowd time to buy ice cream,' the new captain of the trapeze pointed out. 'I'd rather not send someone home with a broken back — bad for publicity, don't you think?' It was clear that he had little respect for their ringmaster and the way he disregarded their safety.

Drago himself took over the ring after the interval, demonstrating his skills with his whip. A bull was sent into the ring, snorting and stamping its feet, only to find itself lassoed and helpless in seconds as the clowns ran in to drag it away. He then showed a second skill, plucking a lighted cigarette from the lips of a clown who ran off screaming. Whether this was for show or if he was genuinely hurt, no one knew.

Finally, it was time for Beppo to show his paces. As there wasn't a vacant seat, Rosalie crept down to the front of the ring and crouched on the lowest step, hugging her knees. Although her heart was thudding in her chest and she didn't like to be sitting so close to the action and the fire, she knew

Beppo would feel much better if he knew she was there. She had a few sweet apples in her pockets to give to him afterwards. The little horse didn't look at all like himself today — Edmond had trimmed his luxuriant mane and tied up his tail to lessen the risk of their catching fire. Edmond himself looked very different, too. Dressed in a glittering pale green costume, he resembled a woodland elf, his riotous curls contained in a band at the nape of his neck. He smiled at Rosalie and gave her a thumbs-up but she knew he was feeling just as anxious as she was. They would both be glad when this part of the show was over.

The little circus orchestra struck up with soft yet exciting music, suggesting the drama about to take place and Edmond rode Beppo into the ring to jump through the hoops he had cleared with such ease during practice. The only difference was that this time Drago remained in the ring, cracking the whip from time to time, supposedly to encourage the little pony. But, each time he did this, Rosalie winced, wishing he'd stop. She didn't want the little horse to be frightened and lose concentration. But at last the moment was here; it was time for the real thing.

Several clowns rushed in, setting fire to the three rings, lighting up the whole scene with a hissing sound, making a spectacular show of smoke and flame and producing a chorus of oohs and ahs from the crowd. The music stepped up a beat, increasing the drama and a third clown stood by with buckets of water.

Having learned to trust Edmond implicitly, Beppo gathered speed and Rosalie clasped her hands in prayer, holding her breath as he took the first hoop without mishap, making the crowd cheer. She felt as if she had jumped it with him.

Gaining confidence and settling into his rhythm, the little horse jumped through the second hoop which was higher. Rosalie started to breathe again; it was going to be all right.

But at the third hoop which was much larger and higher, everything went wrong. One of the clowns decided to mix up the action, giving a loud whoop and starting to juggle some balls at the side of the ring. Drago, annoyed by this intervention during what was to have been the highlight of the act, glared at the clown and cracked his whip as an order for him to desist. But he didn't take enough care to see where the end of his whip might land. It struck Edmond a stinging blow on the back of the neck, breaking the band and releasing his mass of hair just at the moment Beppo tried to leap through the last ring of fire.

With his rider distracted, Beppo mistimed the jump and fell into the fiery hoop, bringing the ring, himself and his rider — whose hair was on fire — crashing to the ground. Edmond gave a raw scream and fell silent, mercifully knocked unconscious by the fall. The fire spread at once to the straw beside the dusty old curtains the performers used to come in and out of the ring, and quickly ignited the side of the tent itself. Fanned by the breeze, the fire licked up the sides until the big top itself was ablaze, causing widespread panic in the audience. Parents snatched up their weeping, frightened children and ran for the exits, pushing, shoving and almost causing the tent to collapse in their anxiety to be the first away from the flames. A woman and a small child fell and were trampled by the crowd.

The clown with the buckets of water just stood there as if frozen, rooted to the spot. He remembered himself only when his companions snatched the buckets away from him, using them in an attempt to stop the spread of the blaze. Fire extinguishers took care of the rest but too late; the damage was already done. Most of the people in that audience would never visit a circus again.

Concerned only for Edmond and Beppo,

Rosalie was scarcely aware of all this as she pulled off her jacket and rushed into the ring to wrap it around Edmond's head to put out the flames, gritting her teeth against the heat that was still intense enough to scorch her hands. Even as she did so, she could see how badly Edmond's face had been burned; he might even lose his sight — certainly he would never have the face of an angel again. Mercifully, he was still unconscious. His clothing, covered in glittering plastic stars, was burned into his flesh and she knew better than to try taking it off.

Sensing Drago's presence, she looked up at him, expecting to see some sign of concern for Edmond's plight. Instead, she saw only a sulky expression, his lips pursed in annoyance.

'What a shambles,' he muttered. 'So this is what we get — after all my hard work. We'll never get that sponsor to deal with us now.'

'You selfish bastard!' Rosalie stood up and yelled at him. 'Can't you see what you've done? Don't you care?'

'How dare you speak to me — ' Drago began.

'Oh, I dare.' Despising him as she did, she wasn't afraid of him now. 'Call an ambulance, damn you! Can't you see how badly this man is injured? He might even be dying.'

When Drago continued to glare at her, Rosalie didn't bother to argue. She knew where he kept his mobile phone and snatched it from his pocket to dial emergency services.

By now, the rest of the circus performers were gathering round, including Cleo and Cassia, finally aware of the seriousness of this event. Cleo even brought a rug while they waited for the ambulance.

'He'll need that,' she said in a voice husky with tears. 'For the shock.' She raised a hand to her trembling mouth. 'Oh, Edmond!'

Only now this had happened did Rosalie realize how popular the little man had been with the circus folk. *Had been?* Was she writing him off as if he were already dead?

It was only when she could see there was no more to do for Edmond other than await the arrival of the ambulance, that she turned to see how Beppo had fared. The little pony lay where he had fallen, his eyes rolled back in his head. She could see no serious injury apart from superficial burns on his legs but he was very still. Rosalie, who had lived with horses all her life, knew death when she saw it. It had all been too much for the elderly Shetland who had suffered a massive heart attack. He would never eat the apples she had in her pocket and she would never bury her face in his sweet-smelling mane again.

By now the paramedics had arrived to attend to Edmond. Having stabilized him as best they could, they were giving him oxygen and preparing to lift him into the ambulance. Rosalie stepped forward, wanting to ask if she could go with them but was surprised to see Cleo step up instead, wearing a coat to hide her costume as one of the paramedics offered a hand to help her aboard. Feeling bereft and unable to stop the tears rolling down her face, Rosalie could only watch as the ambulance moved off, taking her friend away. He was in good hands now and she could only hope he would be all right.

'You didn't know, did you?' Cassia spoke up beside her. 'Cleo and Edmond have been lovers for years. They kept it quiet as they didn't want Drago to know. Although I have a nasty feeling that he did.'

'Oh,' was all Rosalie could say. What a fool she had been to think she was Edmond's only friend just because he was the whole world to her; the only one to show her any real kindness. Suddenly, she looked around for Drago, her grief finally overtaken by rage.

'This is all your fault!' she ranted at him. 'You did this — making them take part in that dangerous act!'

'Oh, take a pill — go and lie down.' Drago tried to wave her away. 'I've enough to worry about over damage control without your hysterics as well.'

Infuriated by his calm, dismissive attitude, Rosalie screamed and kicked him in the shins as hard as she could. She needed a reaction. Any reaction. It was swift in coming.

Drago bunched his gloved fist and drew back, punching her in the face with the full force of it, knocking her to the ground. He would have gone in to do more damage but several of the clowns held him back.

'Let her be. She's just a kid,' one of them said, horrified by Drago's brutality to his own child.

'You've been nothing but trouble since I set eyes on you.' Drago still glared at her. 'You'll be the ruin of me and I'm sorry I found you.'

'No more sorry than I am,' she managed to croak through the blood in her mouth. The world was still spinning and her cheek hurt so much, she wondered if he'd broken a bone in her face.

Surprisingly, it was Cassia who gathered her up and supported her into the trailer she shared with her sister. She bathed Rosalie's cheek and found ice to bring down the swelling. Gently, she felt around to see if anything was broken.

'Good job he was wearing gloves,' she said. 'And luckily you've got strong bones. I think you've got away with it.'

'Why are you being so nice to me?' Rosalie said at last. 'I thought you and Cleo hated me.'

'Oh, hate is a big word,' Cassia said. 'We were more angry with Drago than you. Telling us we were over the hill. Bringing in his pretty teenaged daughter to take our place.'

'I just wanted to work with you,' Rosalie whispered. 'Not take your place.'

'Drago can be quite evil at times. I think he sowed the seeds for this disaster a while ago which makes me think he knew all along about Edmond and Cleo. He knows there's a jealous streak in her and he was always whispering in her ear, telling her he thought Edmond fancied you.'

'No, never,' Rosalie felt bound to protest. 'He was kind to me, that's all.'

'And when Cleo saw him putting an arm around you that day and leading you up the steps to his trailer — well, it seemed to confirm her worst fears.'

'It wasn't like that, not at all. There was never anything creepy in Edmond's behaviour to me — he thinks of me as a child and was comforting me because my father had been a bit harsh.'

'Oh, I believe you although Cleo wouldn't.

Drago wanted her to believe the worst of Edmond in the hope of breaking them up. He used to call Edmond a malformed freak and certainly wouldn't have wanted him for a brother-in-law.' Cassia sighed. 'Before Cleo left in the ambulance she said she was tired of pretending. If Edmond recovers from this, she's going to marry him, whatever Drago says.'

'Even if he should be blind?' Rosalie said softly, remembering what the halo of fire had done to the little man's face.

At that moment the door to the trailer was thrown open and Cleo burst into the room, sobbing violently. Rosalie and Cassia stared at her. They hadn't expected her back so soon.

'Oh, Cassia! Cassia!' Cleo threw herself into her sister's arms. 'He's gone. They did all they could but he died on the way to the hospital. My lovely Edmond is dead.'

Rosalie couldn't prevent a small cry of grief, making Cleo turn and glare at her.

'What's this, Cassia?' she said. 'Why is this little bitch in here polluting the atmosphere?'

'Hush, Cleo.' Cassia tried to smooth her sister's hair from her face except Cleo pushed her hand away to glare at Rosalie. 'I can explain everything.'

'Better make it good, then. You know what Drago said. She's been all over Edmond for weeks, trying to seduce him.'

'Rubbish,' Cassia said. 'Don't believe a word of it. You only have to look at her. I know she's tall but she's still just a kid — too young to think of seducing anyone, let alone a man as sophisticated as Edmond.'

All the same, Cleo continued to watch Rosalie through narrowed eyes and when she spoke, her voice was deep with malice.

'I wish Drago had never set eyes on you. You and your broken-down Shetland pony. If you hadn't come here, Edmond might still be alive.'

'Oh Cleo, stop,' Cassia tried to intervene. 'You're in shock and don't know what you're saying. This isn't Rosalie's fault. Blame Drago if you want to blame anyone.'

'It always comes back to Drago, doesn't it?' Cleo wouldn't be pacified. 'Our handsome baby brother who has nothing but a black hole where his heart ought to be. If only that fool Josefina hadn't tried to trap him by getting pregnant,' — she paused to stab an accusing finger at Rosalie — 'this little bitch wouldn't be alive to trouble us at all.'

Cassia rubbed her sister's back, trying to calm her. 'Cleo, don't. You're just torturing yourself. The world is full of regrets about what might have been.'

'I might have been happy once. And

Edmond might still be alive,' Cleo wailed and fell down on her bed, giving way to a fresh storm of tears.

'I'm sorry,' Cassia whispered to Rosalie, 'but I think you should go. She can't think past her grief at present.'

'It's OK.' Rosalie rose shakily from the chair she'd been sitting in. 'Thank you for — '

'It was nothing. And keep that ice with you — your face is still swollen.'

Rosalie went on legs that still felt unsteady, scarcely noticing the sudden absence of people around the circus camp. Tonight there was no cheerful camp fire or barbecue, and there were few lights on in any of the trailers. But her face was still throbbing and she was feeling too miserable to wonder where everyone was.

It was clear to her what she needed to do. She had no intention of staying with this cruel man who was her father. He had never cared for her. For the first time in her life she could choose her own path. Thanks to the clown she had earned enough money to please herself. She would buy a train or bus ticket and find her way to Rome where she would look for work. She would take anything she could get and would clean public toilets if need be. She'd had enough practice after all, cleaning up after humans and animals here.

But she had a bad feeling as soon as she entered the trailer she shared with that other girl. She could see at a glance that it had been stripped bare. Nothing remained that wasn't tied down. Rosalie's few possessions were gone, including the small silver frame containing the only photograph she had of her mother. Her bed had been roughly pulled apart and there was a gaping hole in the mattress where her money had been. Even the few new clothes she had bought for herself had been taken; only her old, shabby jeans and a couple of shapeless T-shirts remained. Too shocked and exhausted to weep, she lay down on the bed and put the remains of the melting ice on her swollen face. Her eye had almost closed and there would be an enormous bruise in the morning. Everyone would see what Drago had done.

She was just as desperate and helpless as when Drago first collected her from the farm but now she was much worse off, having lost her belief in human nature along with her only friend. If Mancia were here, she would fall to her knees to say a prayer for Edmond's immortal soul but Rosalie didn't believe in all that. Even less so after what happened. She could only hope the little man continued to exist somewhere and had gone to a better place.

She might have made friends with Cassia but she knew Cleo wouldn't allow it. So here she was — fifteen years old and alone in the world except for a father who wanted only to exploit her and use her to his best advantage whether she liked it or not. Without money, escape was impossible. She was unhappy, miserable and had absolutely no idea what to do.

4

Drago didn't show his face until well after eleven the following morning. Usually so careful of his appearance, making sure he was washed and groomed before showing himself to the world, he didn't care that he was red-eyed, unkempt and unshaven as he squinted against the cold light of day, surveying the wreckage of what should have been his ticket to a better life. Last night he had locked himself in his van with a bottle of whisky, safe in the knowledge that the clowns, who also acted as roustabouts, would rally round and clear up the physical aspects of the mess. Financially, he knew it would not be so easy.

In Ernesto's day, although the premiums were heavy, the circus had always carried insurance but when Drago received the latest request for payment and seeing the premium was larger than ever, he had chosen to ignore it. Instead, he had spent the money on a larger tent and a new trapeze.

There had been some heavy showers in the night, adding water to the damage already done by the fire. Surveying the scene in the morning, he could see at a glance that the clowns had done nothing and must have spent the evening drowning their sorrows instead. The tent still leaned at an unsafe angle, a huge hole burned in one side. The stands remained as they were last night, broken or overturned. And where was everyone? The trapeze artistes had voted with their feet, disappearing like mist in the early morning. Empty space remained where their vehicles had been standing and Drago suspected they had stolen his new equipment in lieu of being paid. There was no joyful barking from the performing dogs as more than half the clowns had left, taking their little companions with them. They had even stolen some of the smaller vans, well aware that Drago couldn't afford to pursue them. There remained only the big prime mover and its decorated trailer, used to transport the big top and the collapsible stands. The prancing horses looked absurdly cheerful in the wake of such disaster. The sisters' horse float also remained, together with their luxury American Winnebago. Fortunately for them they'd had the sense to think ahead, spending their money on something practical that would improve their lifestyle. They knew better than to leave money in a savings account for Drago to beg or borrow. There remained also one or two of the older vans, occupied by the clowns who had decided to stay and there was also the ticket office trailer and Rosalie's little van. It was obvious that with such limited resources, it wouldn't be possible to put on a show.

Drago rubbed his face that itched from his overindulgence of the night before and closed his eyes, hoping that when he opened them again the scene would have changed. How could everything fall apart so quickly in just one night? He didn't even know if he had enough drivers to move the circus on. And this was an urgent need, before the townspeople turned up in force, demanding their money back. He groaned. There were too many problems all coming at him at once and the brilliant sunshine hurt his eyes. He knew only one thing for sure — the circus must leave here as soon as possible.

'About time you showed your face, Mr Ringmaster,' Cleo tackled him as soon as he left his trailer. 'We need a bit of leadership here.' Her sharp words felt like nails being hammered into his skull as she snapped her fingers in front of his face. 'Look lively! You're always sounding off about being in charge, so you need to step up and find us a way out of this mess.'

'Christ, woman. Give me a chance,' he

muttered. 'Where is everyone?'

'Gone. Those that had sense enough, anyway.'

'All right,' Drago said, massaging his throbbing temples. 'Get Cassia. My trailer now. Family conference.'

'Great.' Cleo folded her arms, not about to let him off the hook. 'You call us a pair of old hags, you fetch that ignorant farm girl to replace us and now you want a family conference, expecting us to help and advise you. Well, you dug this hole for yourself, little brother, so now you can worm your way out of it.'

'Cleo, have a heart. I need some coffee before I can think about anything.'

'So I'll make you coffee,' she said, bustling towards the trailer she shared with Cassia. 'And we'll have the family conference in the Winnebago. I'm not sitting in your smelly abode that reeks of stale booze.' The vixen was back on form. This morning she showed no sign of being the grief-stricken woman of the night before. Cleo didn't believe in crying over spilt milk. Her feelings had been packed up and hidden away until she could bear to look at them again.

'Where's Rosalie this morning?' Drago muttered, half hoping she'd taken off with the clowns and their dogs. 'Anyone seen her?'

Cleo and Cassia shrugged.

'Still in her trailer, I think,' Cassia said. 'Recovering from that punch in the face that you gave her.'

Drago winced. 'She disrespected me and I lost my temper. All the same, I shouldn't have hit her so hard.'

Cleo and Cassia raised their eyebrows, exchanging glances. This was the first time they'd heard Drago admit to being wrong about anything.

With coffee and toast in front of them, Cleo was all business. 'Honesty time,' she said. 'Realistically, how much money do we have left?'

'Enough to get away from the outskirts of Rome,' Drago said. 'The trapeze artistes took off without being paid. That's a bonus at least. Although they took all the new equipment instead.'

'And do we have any savings?' Cassia asked. 'Aside from last night's box office?'

Drago hesitated before answering her. 'Some,' he said, frowning and rubbing his nose.

'Come on, this is honesty time, remember?' Cleo snapped.

'No, we don't,' he said. 'I had a sponsor almost hooked — but he won't be interested now, not after last night's shambles.'

'Maybe it's time for us to split up. Cassia and I can always hire ourselves and our horses to another troupe.'

'And you'd leave me out on a limb, all alone?' Drago moaned. 'A ringmaster without any acts?'

Cleo shrugged. 'Why shouldn't we? There's never been any love lost between us. We're only half related, if that.'

Drago thought it best to ignore that remark. 'With no sponsor on the horizon, I was thinking of going to Uncle Angelo.' He really didn't have any ideas and was throwing this in out of desperation. He wasn't surprised when both the sisters laughed.

'Angelo Barcelona?' Cassia said eventually. 'He gives me the creeps. Anyone less like an angel I've yet to meet. A drug dealer and God knows what else — a gangster, no less. And he lives halfway up a mountain in Sicily — the other end of the country from here. I'd sound him out first if I were you. Save yourself a wasted journey.'

'I can't do that. It's too easy for him to say no on the phone or the internet. He'll find it harder if we're talking face to face, man to man.'

'You've got some nerve, fronting up to Angelo. He scares the hell out of me and I take some scaring,' Cleo said, giving a small shudder. 'What do you have to offer him anyway, aside from some clapped-out circus trailers with bald tyres? Why should he want to invest in our failing business? No. You need a good bargaining chip to go dealing with Angelo and I don't think you have one.'

'That's where you're wrong. I have a really good bargaining chip to tempt him.' Drago nodded, looking smug as his sisters waited for him to go on. 'I have Rosalie.'

'Rosalie!' the sisters said in chorus, before convulsing with laughter yet again.

'What?' Drago scowled at them. 'She's young. She's untouched — unless of course Edmond — '

'Don't go there,' Cassia said, hearing her sister's indrawn breath. 'You know very well that he didn't.'

'An untouched virgin then, in this day and age. Has to be worth something to someone.' Drago spread his hands.

'You're a piece of work, aren't you Drago?' Cassia folded her arms. 'You'd sell your own daughter to a life of vice, as long as you can get out from under.'

'I think you're kidding yourself.' Cleo gave him a pitying look. 'Angelo won't pay you for Rosalie. If he needs new blood for his rackets, he can gather all the teenaged runaways he needs from the train and bus stations. He has pretty-boy scouts hanging out there on a day-to-day basis, picking up lost girls.'

'Not as pretty as Rosalie or certified virgins.'

'She might not be so pretty now,' Cassia couldn't resist teasing him. 'After you knocked out a few teeth when you smashed up her face.'

'Oh God, I didn't, did I?' Drago groaned.

'And this is really your best idea?' Cleo shook her head, showing she wasn't convinced.

'Not my best — it's my only idea.' Once more Drago spread his hands.

Cleo considered this for a moment. 'Well, there was always that old rumour that you were Angelo's son and not Pop's,' she said at last, making Cassia gasp. Obviously, this was the first she'd heard of it. Drago grinned and shrugged, having heard that rumour himself many times.

'Surely not. That's disgusting,' Cassia said. 'You're suggesting that Angelo was sleeping with Loma? His own sister?'

'Well, Pop's son and heir turned up pretty smartly after the wedding, didn't he? Good going for a man of his age. People were saying Loma had a bun in the oven before Pops married her. No fool like an old fool, eh?'

'Hold on,' Drago said. 'That's my mother

you're talking about. I'm Ernesto's legitimate son, not Angelo's bastard.'

'You might find it suits you better to be Angelo's bastard now.' Cleo screwed up her eyes. 'No need to pussyfoot around it. Loma and Pop can't argue the toss, they're both dead. Grow up and call a spade a spade. Incest goes on in the best of families. Why take risks with a stranger when you can get all the pleasure you need from someone you've grown up with and trust?'

'Cleo!' Cassia said, looking shocked.

'It happens more often than you think. People don't like to talk about it, that's all.' Cleo flapped a hand at her brother. 'You only have to look at him. He's tall, well-built and good-looking like Angelo, while we're both on the short side and have sharp, pointy features like Pops.'

'This is all old news — to me, anyway.' Drago was growing impatient with this diversion. 'We need to solve the problem we have today — to find a way out of this mess.'

'Go and see Angelo, then,' Cleo said. 'You might appeal to his better nature — if he has one. Take your daughter and go on your own; it makes no sense for us all to travel to Sicily. See how the land lies with Angelo and play it by ear. He might be thrilled to know he's a grandfather — far as I know he has no other heirs. Cass and I will hole up at the farm where we usually sit out the winter. We can recruit some more clowns and work up some new acts while you're gone. But don't leave us in limbo forever. I want you to keep in touch regularly and tell us what's happening on a daily basis.'

'OK.' Drago was frankly surprised she had accepted his plan so easily.

'And you'd better take our Winnebago,' Cleo added. 'You'll look too desperate if you turn up in that crappy old van of yours. It will also be more reliable on a long journey.'

'Oh Cleo, no. Not our lovely Winnebago.' Cassia looked close to tears.

'He can borrow it just for this journey,' Cleo persisted. 'We shan't need it while we're at the farm.'

'I suppose.' Cassia said no more, suddenly aware that her sister's eyebrows were writhing and there was some hidden agenda here. 'Never known *you* to be a soft touch before.'

'So that's settled, Drago. You're taking our van to Sicily,' Cleo said. 'But make damned sure you bring it back to us in one piece. And keep in touch regularly or you might find the cops on your doorstep because I've reported it stolen.'

'Oh, Cleo, you wouldn't,' Cassia said.

'Try me.'

'OK. OK.' Drago sighed, weary of all these expectations. 'Just remember I'm the one in the firing line, going cap in hand to Uncle Angelo.'

'And so you should.' Cleo felt bound to have the last word. 'Angelo is *your* uncle, not ours. And it's your fault that Edmond is dead. You and your rings of fire!'

'Enough already, woman.' Drago was still feeling fragile after drowning his sorrows with whisky the night before. 'You're relentless.'

'And I'm not finished yet. You're the ringmaster and supposed to be in charge of things, so it's your job to persuade Luca and the rest of the clowns to stay.'

Drago winced. 'Ah no, can't you talk to them?'

'No. Those guys are old-fashioned — some of them Greek — they don't like doing business with women.'

* * *

Drago found Luca and his friends digging a grave for Beppo on the outskirts of a nearby piece of woodland, wanting to finish the task before Rosalie saw them. In this hot weather, the little horse was already a magnet for flies. Luca made Drago wait until they were done, wiping sweat from his brow as he leaned on his shovel after patting down the gravel on top of the body.

'I know why you're here,' he said, without preamble. 'You want us to move the circus on before the townspeople turn out in force to stone us. Lucky for you, it's a Sunday and they're all in church.'

'It's your livelihood as well as mine,' Drago reminded him. 'I need to find us a new sponsor and drum up some new acts.'

'I've already lost half my workforce,' Luca said. 'Those that remain will have to do twice as much. We'll need to be paid.'

'You will be. Just as soon as I can — '

'No. I don't want to hear any promises you can't keep. We'll want paying up front. Half of last night's box office — now. And don't try to cheat me as I sold most of the tickets.'

Drago was shocked. 'But that's all I have. And I'll need it to look good and talk the talk to get a new sponsor.'

'Your problem — not mine.' Luca shrugged. 'Half of last night's box office or we walk. Take it or leave it.'

'How do I know you won't take off with my vehicles and I'll never see you again?'

'You don't. You'll have to trust me.' And he laughed, watching Drago scowl. 'You have a poor opinion of most people, don't you? We could have left last night with the others, if we wanted to go.'

'All right, all right. It's a deal.' Drago shook hands with bad grace. He hated to part with so much of his dwindling resources but he could see no alternative, although he knew Cleo was sure to give him a hard time.

As it happened, Cleo had other things on her mind. She had called at the hospital mortuary to ask about Edmond in the hope of arranging his funeral, only to find that another woman had beaten her to it. A tiny woman, very similar to Edmond himself, and who was claiming to be his wife. Shocked by this information, Cleo dashed outside just in time to see the little woman, grim-faced but dry-eyed as she watched Edmond's coffin being loaded into a hearse. The undertaker closed the back doors against it and opened the passenger door for her to get into the seat beside him.

Knowing better than to intrude, Cleo could only watch as they drove away, realizing she would never know the answers to the questions seething in her mind. This woman must have been notified as Edmond's next of kin. Was she still legally married to him or had they been divorced? Why had he never trusted her with the real details of his life?

She knew many people joined a circus as a means of running away from their lives but Edmond had always seemed so straightforward, honest and sincere. She sighed. Ever practical, she knew there was nothing more she could do for him now. She wouldn't even have to pay for his funeral.

'Well?' Cassia looked up from her iPad as Cleo jumped back into the driver's seat of the Winnebago. 'That didn't take as long as I thought.'

'No,' Cleo said. 'His relatives were there first — already taken charge of the body.'

'But didn't you introduce yourself? As Edmond's fiancée, you have certain rights. You should have — '

'Do stop rattling, Cassia,' Cleo snapped. 'I didn't — I haven't and you're giving me a headache.'

'I'm sorry. But don't you even want to go to the funeral?'

'What for?' Cleo turned on her, fierce as ever. 'It's not going to bring Edmond back. I wanted a living, breathing man, not a corpse.' Blinded by tears, she started up the Winnebago, driving erratically from the hospital grounds. 'We might as well get Luca to take the big semi and go straight to the farm.'

'Yes,' Cassia said, alarmed by her sister's

fury. 'But I think you'd better let me drive just now.'

★ ★ ★

Ernesto's retreat had been chosen well. Accessible only up winding dirt roads that were poorly marked, his farm was a rambling, solidly constructed farmhouse in a country area not too far from Rome. It lacked many of the modern conveniences most people take for granted but, as circus people are used to a lifestyle of camping, the old boss could see no reason for them to be pampered at his home. Although the farm was reached by a high, winding road, there was a plateau of solid rock where the big semi-trailer and other vans could be parked.

Water was plentiful, coming from a natural spring to several wells and because people used it wisely and economically, they had never dried up. Seasonal vegetables were freely available, grown by Ernesto's gardener and housekeeper; an elderly married couple who lived there full-time. Anything else his visitors wanted, they must provide for themselves as they did on the road.

The first thing Cleo and Cassia did on arrival was check on their horses, making sure they had travelled well.

Rosalie, avoiding Drago as much as possible, had travelled with Luca. Her face looked painful and badly bruised, although it didn't hurt so much now the colour of the bruise was coming out. Unhappy as he was to see this vulnerable girl in such a sorry state, Luca knew better than to draw attention to it. She stared out of the side window, seeing nothing, and he knew she was grieving for the loss of Edmond and also for the little pony that had been part of her life for almost as long as she could remember.

'We're going to a beautiful part of Italy. Do you know it?' Luca said, hoping to draw her into conversation.

'No,' she said listlessly. And then more vehemently, 'I don't care where I am or where I go. Life is nothing to me now.'

'Ah, you say that because you are young and this is the first pain you have ever experienced.'

'If that's what you think, you don't know me at all,' she snapped, sitting with folded arms and turning away from him.

'Good,' Luca said, smiling. 'Anger is better than apathy. Soon you will be able to feel again.'

'I don't want to. Life hurts.'

'Well, of course it does. How can you appreciate the good times if nothing bad ever happens?'

She glared at him. 'Where do you find your philosophies, Luca? Christmas crackers?'

'Ouch!' Luca laughed. 'I think I deserved that.'

This produced a ghost of a smile from Rosalie.

'You see? You're smiling again. You haven't forgotten how to laugh.'

5

'Why do I have to go with you?' Rosalie was surprised as well as suspicious when she heard that Drago wanted her to accompany him on the long journey to Sicily. She knew she sounded like a typical teenager, cross and sulky, but she didn't care. 'I'm sure you'd sooner take one of your women — not me.'

'I don't have any women — not now,' Drago started to say until he realized he didn't have to explain himself to this chit of a girl. Her bruise was still faintly visible with discolouration beneath her eye but, fortunately, Cassia had lied about the missing teeth. Rosalie's good teeth were all in place although they were barely seen as her smiles were rare. 'If I want you to accompany me on this journey, that's what you'll do. And if I need a home-cooked meal while we're out on the road, I'll expect you to prepare it.'

'I can't cook.' Rosalie continued to pout.

'And tuck in that lip before you fall over it.' Drago shrugged. 'Open some tins then. Any fool can do that.'

'I still don't see why I have to go.' Rosalie continued to sulk because she'd been looking

97

forward to some time for herself, away from his critical presence. 'I'm used to farm life and I'd much rather stay here. But I suppose you're tired of me hanging around and cramping your lifestyle so you're thinking of dumping me somewhere — like those other girls.'

'Those other girls weren't my daughter.' He mustered what he hoped was a winning smile. 'Besides, on a long journey like this, we'll have time to get to know one another properly.'

'You think?' She looked at him from under her eyelashes, doubting his sincerity.

The truth was that since Edmond and Beppo died, she no longer cared what happened to her; she felt like a rudderless boat carried aimlessly by the tide. She hadn't yet found the courage to tell Luca that the money he worked so hard to obtain for her had been stolen. And she had lost more than just money — she had lost the possibility of freedom and independence as well.

Luca had been concerned when Drago announced that everyone was to remain here while Rosalie would be the only one to accompany him on his journey to Sicily.

'I'm sure there's a lot more to this than he says,' he confided to Cassia. 'I know Rosalie's his daughter but it's obvious that they don't like one another. So why make her go on this cross-country journey where they'll be forced into each other's company for several days? Like any teenager, she can be sulky and difficult. What if she annoys him and he hits her again?'

Cassia shrugged, not trusting herself to say anything. She was all too aware of Drago's reason for taking Rosalie to Sicily and she didn't like it, either. She kept telling herself it would be all right; Angelo might be delighted to have a new granddaughter.

'Well, say something.' Luca was still waiting for some sort of response. 'Give me your thoughts at least.'

'I don't have any,' Cassia said. 'As you know I have very little influence where my brother and sister are concerned.'

Luca regarded her, head on one side. 'Now why does that sound like a cop-out?'

'Luca, I can't tell you anything. Our finances are in a mess and Drago needs to prise some money out of Angelo or we're done for. Right now we have bigger things on our minds than what might happen to Rosie.'

'Ah. So you do expect something to happen to her?'

'I don't know anything!' Cassia was obviously flustered and anxious to get away. 'You just have to trust me.'

'I hate it when people say that because it usually means they have something to hide,' Luca said. 'I don't expect much of those two.' He nodded towards Cleo and Drago. 'But I thought you, at least, would have some compassion and care for the kid.'

'Stop trying to make me feel guilty when it isn't my fault. Can't you see I have trouble enough, trying to care for myself?' And with that, she turned and ran back to the stables, hiding her trembling mouth with her hand and blinded by the hot tears that she didn't want him to see.

Another week was to pass before Drago finally set off for Sicily with Rosalie. He wanted to make sure her bruises had faded and that she had benefited from the good food provided at the farm. She would have liked to prolong her mourning and starve but the fresh food was too tempting and she was a growing girl.

When the day of departure finally came, Drago set off sedately, trying to drive smoothly. He knew Cleo would be watching until they were out of sight, fearing the worst and already regretting her decision to let him take the Winnebago. But if he hoped to impress Uncle Angelo and get him to finance a new venture, it wouldn't do to turn up poverty-stricken and desperate, in a broken-down van with bald tyres.

When he turned a corner and disappeared from sight, Cleo gave her sister a slap on the shoulder and grinned before laughing richly. 'Oh ha, ha. Good riddance at last to both of them. I'll be very surprised if we ever see Drago, his daughter or that Winnebago again.'

'You don't think he'll succeed with Angelo, then?' Cassia stared at her, puzzled.

'Not a snowball's chance in hell. You know Drago — King Midas's idiot brother — everything he touches turns to shit. And I know Angelo, too. He has pots of money and doesn't part with it easily. But at the very least Drago will be out of our hair for a week or so, giving us time to make other arrangements for ourselves without him trying to horn in and take over everything.'

'But Cleo, I don't understand. If that's what you were thinking, why on earth did you let him take our van?'

'Because it's the only one that will get him to Sicily without breaking down.' She chuckled. 'And, just between ourselves, that van isn't ours any more. I took the precaution of refinancing it over a week ago.'

Cassia stared at her open-mouthed. 'Without telling me? I can't believe you did that.'

'Because I know you. You can't keep a

secret to save your life.'

'But — '

'I wish I could be there to see Drago's face. He'll have such a surprise when the payments aren't met and the finance company send in some heavies to pick it up.'

'But Cleo, that's a terrible thing to do! Never mind Drago — what about Rosalie? What will happen to her?'

'Who cares?' Cleo shrugged. 'She's his daughter, after all. Nothing to us.'

'And just how long have you been planning all this, without telling me?'

'Long enough. With the circus ruined and Edmond gone, I knew we'd have to fend for ourselves. Some time ago I met this Australian guy, Tarquin — a circus groupie with more money than sense as well. He's followed us everywhere but I've always played hard to get to keep him interested. He has good contacts both here and overseas and already loves our act. He's desperate to hire the pair of us and our horses. He might even take us back to Australia with him. I knew that if Drago found out, he'd try to take over the deal but this one's just for us. With Drago out of the picture, I was going to ask Luca to join us, we'll need some reliable people of our own, too.'

'He already knows something's up. He's been grilling me.'

'Well, you can tell him everything now. And when baby brother comes back — if he ever does — you and I will be long gone and he won't know where to find us.'

'Whew.' Cassia blew out a long breath. 'Don't do things by halves, do you, sis? Let's hope Uncle Angelo takes to Rosalie.'

Cleo rolled her eyes. 'I wish you'd stop worrying about that girl. She'll land on her feet all right — the pretty ones always do.'

★ ★ ★

Irritated with her father for bringing her away from the farm where she was at last beginning to enjoy life again, Rosalie spent a lot of the time in sulky silence. She avoided conversation by lying on Cassia's bed in the back of the van, listening to music. Cassia had left her an old portable DVD player with headphones so that, for some of the time at least, she could forget that Drago was there at all. She did know how to cook simple meals but she wasn't about to let him know. It amused her to watch him grimace over the burnt offerings she brought to the table from the portable gas stove, filling the van with an acrid smoke that clung to the curtains. Cleo would have something to say about that when they returned. After a particularly disastrous meal of burnt sausages, Drago suggested that since Rosalie had wasted the food, she might use some of her own money to buy them supper at a bistro, forcing her to tell him how she had been robbed. She wasn't entirely sure he believed her but she didn't care. Following that, they lived on pizza and other takeaways.

Although her father wasn't the best of travelling companions, in some ways Rosalie wished for the journey never to end. In no time at all she got used to the comfort of lying in Cassia's bed with the luxury of fine linen around her. Drago rarely engaged her in conversation and left her to mind the van while he went drinking alone or met up with people he knew along the way. And she still didn't know why he had brought her on this journey to Sicily. He never bothered to involve her in anything so why hadn't he left her behind with everyone else at the farm?

Deprived of her usual busy lifestyle, she had been filling out quickly, beginning to gain a little weight. Fortunately, it was in all the right places. She had always been tall for her age and used to stoop to compensate, looking awkward and heron-like, but now she was developing breasts. When they stopped at a service station and she jumped down from the van, shaking out her unusual, red-gold hair, she became aware that men's eyes followed her. Experimentally, she would throw back her shoulders and walk tall, sometimes receiving an appreciative growl for her efforts. Pretending to be offended, she would stick her nose in the air and ignore them but in fact she was relishing this newly discovered power over the opposite sex.

But Drago noticed it, too, and disapproved. 'Stop swinging your hips like that — you'll give people the wrong impression. They'll think you're a whore.'

She smiled and said nothing, kissing the air in his direction.

'And you should stop eating so much. You're putting on weight.'

'I'm growing up and becoming a woman, that's all.'

'Well, stop doing it around me. It brings us the wrong sort of attention.'

She considered this for a moment before speaking. 'I think it's time you told me what this is about and why I'm here.' She was trying to sound fearless and confident although she felt as if he could see her heart thumping in her chest. The memory of that vicious punch was still clear in her mind and if he were sufficiently aggravated, he might easily strike her again. 'Tell me more about this uncle of yours. He must be scary as hell if even Cleo's afraid of him. So why do I have to meet him?'

'You think too much into things,' Drago muttered. 'I brought you along because you may be able to help. I want him to finance a new venture for me and Angelo likes bright young things around him, that's all.'

'Sounds like a lame excuse to me. Luca says he's a gangster.'

'Rubbish. Luca doesn't know what he's talking about.'

'And he says you have a hidden agenda and that I should watch my back.'

'Then Luca should learn to mind his own damned business and shut his fat mouth.' A muscle started twitching in Drago's jaw, telling Rosalie she had struck a nerve.

'So what do you have in mind for me really?' Her tone was light, mocking. 'Am I to be sold into white slavery to save the circus?'

This was so uncannily near the truth that Drago tittered nervously. 'What an imagination. What made you say that?'

'Because you never do anything that doesn't benefit yourself.' She folded her arms and smiled at him, shaking her head. 'Silly me. I expected so much of you when you saved me from that life of drudgery with Mancia. How green I was. It was luxury

106

compared to the life I've been living with you, dear Papa. So please be honest for once in your life and tell me your plans. I've learned not to like surprises.'

But Drago had no intention of satisfying her curiosity. Not now, anyway. He ruffled her hair, making her shrink from his touch, saying he needed a drink. This time, he locked her inside the Winnebago before he left.

★ ★ ★

Rosalie enjoyed the journey on the ferry to Messina although she could see that Drago did not; he kept his eyes on the horizon the whole time, longing for the journey to be over. She had not realized until now that he was afraid of the sea, although clearly he didn't wish to talk about it and she didn't raise the question for fear of making him angry yet again.

She didn't ask where they were going when they left the ferry as Drago seemed to know his way around. They took a winding route that seemed to bring them to one of the highest points on the island with magnificent views overlooking the sea. The actual entrance to Angelo's villa was so cleverly concealed, it resembled a country track leading to nowhere, putting her in mind of the farm they had left behind. This family seemed to share a reluctance to be easily found. They drove for at least ten minutes before the villa itself loomed in sight, surrounded by formal gardens and a magnificent fountain with dolphins and mermaids; a massive centrepiece in the circular lawn outside the house.

When she caught sight of the villa for the first time, Rosalie could only gasp, intimidated and overawed. She had never seen such luxury and magnificence at close quarters before, having expected Angelo's villa to be more like a farmhouse than this palace with huge windows all round, statues reminiscent of Michelangelo outside, gargoyles staring down from its walls and wide stone steps, leading up to a pair of magnificent, old-fashioned double doors. She looked down at her shabby T-shirt and jeans, the only clothes her trailer companion had left for her, and wished she had something better to wear. Drago grinned at her and shrugged, aware that she was discomfited.

'Oh yes,' he said, nodding towards the palatial entrance with the classical statues on either side of the door. 'My uncle is wealthy, all right. Almost disgustingly loaded. That's why we're here.'

The door opened as soon as they pulled up

outside it. Closed circuit television must have alerted someone to their arrival. A brutish-looking person, more like a bear than a man, came to look them over before they were permitted to come inside. Drago allowed himself to be patted down as the man searched for weapons and, finding none, he turned his attention to Rosalie.

'Don't you dare touch me,' she said, dreading the thought of those heavy hands moving all over her body. 'I'm not carrying anything. I'm just a kid.'

'OK.' The man smiled, showing surprisingly white teeth. 'You sure know how to spoil a fella's fun.'

'Just let them in, Bruno,' a voice called from behind him, sounding irritated. 'This is my nephew. I've been expecting him.'

'Sorry, Maestro.' The big man backed off immediately, looking chastened. 'You should have said.'

Some moments later, when Bruno had been sent off in search of refreshments, Angelo ushered them into a comfortable sitting room, filled with enough ormolu clocks and antiques in delicate showcases to stock a small shop. There were oil paintings on the walls, coffee tables covered with glossy magazines and as many couches with well-stuffed cushions as a room of that size could hold. Rosalie studied their host, thinking how familiar he looked until she realized he looked just like an older, tougher version of Drago. He had the same arrogant twist to the lips and the same dark eyes that at first glance seemed deceptively soft. His hair was white, while Drago's was only beginning to have touches of grey and, although he must be in his late sixties or early seventies, he had kept the figure of a much younger man. He carried a riding crop, encrusted with stones that must be worth a fortune if they were real. Intuitively, Rosalie knew that they were.

Without troubling to make small talk, Angelo went straight to the heart of the matter.

'So, nephew, I can't believe this is only a social visit. How come I hear nothing of you for months if not years and now here you are on my doorstep, cap in hand and want-ing . . . ? Exactly what is it you want from me, I wonder? Money, I suppose. Everyone does. Always a hazard for an old man who has far too much in his sock.' He nodded towards Rosalie and smiled. 'I suppose this is why you bring this pretty innocent to dandle in front of me?' He surprised her by seizing her chin and turning her face towards the light to see it better. 'Hmm.' He nodded. 'She may be a beauty when she's grown. Pity you didn't provide her with decent clothes.'

Without waiting for Drago to say anything, he went to an old-fashioned bell pull by the fireplace. Almost at once, a little maid appeared, wearing an old-fashioned white apron over her clothes.

'Yessir — the tray's on its way. The coffee won't be long, sir,' she said, clearly afraid of displeasing Angelo.

'It's all right, Trizia, my dear,' the old man said. 'I want you to accompany this young lady and show her the gardens and the lake. Then you can take her to the kitchen and give her whatever refreshment she likes. By the time you've done all that, our discussions should be finished and you can bring her back here.'

'Yessir,' she said, bobbing a curtsy in the old-fashioned way and smiling shyly at Rosalie.

Angelo waited until the girls were well out of earshot before he said anything else.

'Yes,' Drago nodded. 'I saw you assessing her. And, before you ask, I can vouch for it — the girl is untouched.'

'So she should be at her age,' the old man snapped. 'I don't hold with this penchant for paedophilia.'

'Ah,' Drago said, thinking this conversation

wasn't going the way he had hoped. 'So, you wouldn't want her, then? Not even for one of your wealthier clients?'

'What do you take me for? Some kind of pimp?' The old man's face flushed in anger but he paused as Bruno came into the room with some drinks and glasses on a tray. Sensing the atmosphere was less than friendly, the man left immediately, leaving Angelo to serve the drinks himself. Without offering anything to his nephew, Angelo poured himself a large Scotch and drank it in two quick gulps.

'Call me a hypocrite, if you like, because I do have people in my organization used to handling that sort of thing. But I've never liked it. Young girls pressed into a life of vice before they're old enough to know what they're doing.'

'What's wrong, Uncle? Getting squeamish in your old age?'

'I'm getting older now and taking stock of my life. I'm not proud of some of the ways I make money. I've dealt in drugs, in vice and in the latest cash-cow — people smuggling . . . '

Drago began to feel ill. The last thing he wanted to hear was his uncle's expression of regret for the life he had led. He could see already that the journey had been a complete waste of time. Angelo certainly wasn't going to pay him to take Rosalie off his hands. He cursed himself for bringing her here, looking like a street urchin — although money was tight, he should at least have bought her some decent clothes.

'Fact is, Uncle,' he said, clearing a throat that was suddenly dry. 'I was all set with a new tent and trapeze but we had a bit of a disaster. A fire at the circus — and I wanted — that is, I hoped — you'd see your way clear to giving me a loan.'

'A contradiction in terms, my boy. *Give* and *loan* don't belong in the same sentence.' Angelo sighed, shaking his head. 'Lord, help me. What did I ever do to deserve such a useless son?'

'The rumours are true, then?' Drago's hopes rose yet again. 'You're ready to admit that I am your son?'

'Well, of course you are. Do you think that impotent old fool, Ernesto, sired you? That little strutting peacock?' Angelo laughed. 'It suited him well enough to believe so at the time. My father would have killed my sister and I if he'd found out the truth. That's how we came together in the first place. Our mutual terror of the old man. After what we'd been up to, she needed a husband quickly and had always enjoyed the thought of the

113

circus and a life on the road. What is it about circuses that is so irresistible to women? I hear you get more than your share yourself.'

The old man was beginning to soften towards him but Drago was too stupid to see it, money being the only thing on his mind.

'See here, Uncle,' he said, still feeling awkward about calling him father. 'Faustino's Circus would be a good investment for you. With the right acts, we could soon be as big as the Cirque du — '

'Do you really think me such a fool?' Angelo's laughter interrupted him. 'You come here, cap in hand like a gypsy — with nothing. You don't even own that fancy caravan — it belongs to those girls.'

'How did you . . . ?'

'Because I take the trouble to find out such things. Do you think my many businesses and a home such as this arrive by chance?'

'No, of course not,' Drago whispered, realizing Angelo was getting irritated again. Foolishly, he asked the first question that came into his head. 'And — and — who will inherit all this magnificence when you go?'

Angelo chuckled. 'Not you, Circus Boy. I have several other bastards a lot more deserving than you.'

'Not even if I were to tell you that Rosalie's my daughter?'

Angelo reacted swiftly. Without a moment's hesitation, he struck Drago across the face with his riding crop, splitting the skin like a piece of fruit. Surprised by the suddenness of the attack, Drago moaned, clasping a hand to his wounded cheek and feeling the warm blood beginning to seep through his fingers.

'You little piece of shit!' Angelo raged at him. 'How can you stand there smiling and saying you're willing to sell your under-aged daughter into a life of vice? To be used by some man and discarded like a broken toy? And all for what? To save that pathetic little side-show of yours.' Without waiting to hear any more, he went to the door and yelled, 'Bruno! In here! Now!'

As if he had been listening behind the door, Bruno was there on the instant, eyes wide with surprise. He had obviously witnessed the results of Angelo's temper before.

'Get this — this piece of crap out of my house and out of my sight.' Angelo could scarcely look at Drago who was whimpering and nursing his wounded face that was bleeding freely now. 'See that he leaves the premises now and make sure he never comes back.'

'Uncle, no! Please!' Drago sounded like the broken man that he was. 'And anyway, what about Rosalie?'

'Rosalie stays here with me. I wouldn't trust you to take care of a stray dog, let alone the granddaughter of the only woman I ever loved. You don't carry my name and for that at least I am grateful. Get out of my house, you shameful excuse for a man. For me, you have ceased to exist.'

In pain and blinded by tears that were all for himself, Drago felt himself hustled to the front door and unceremoniously tossed down the steps. He fell heavily on the gravel below, grazing and bruising his knees. When he felt able to stand again, he staggered towards the Winnebago which remained where he'd left it, opposite the front door, searching for the keys in his pocket.

Once inside, he examined his face and saw that it needed stitches. He might even be scarred for life. Vain as ever, he thought it would make him look dangerous and still more irresistible to women. But for now he must get out of here and reassess his life. He needed money, too. Right now he hadn't enough to get back to the farm — even if it was worth the effort. He had failed, just as the sisters said he would and by now they would be getting on with their lives without him. Even Rosalie was lost to him, stolen by Angelo. He drove slowly away from the villa, going over that last conversation and wishing he had handled the old man with more tact. Too late now.

He drove slowly along the narrow, hazardous mountain track towards the main road and the ferries, knowing it would be wise to leave Sicily as soon as he could. Lost in his own dismal thoughts, he gave little attention to the battered-looking car coming up behind him until the driver forced him on to the wrong side of the road towards the cliff edge. He could see the waves below and that terrified him. He had always been unreasonably afraid of the sea. He slowed down and moved back to the right side of the road, indicating the car should pass, expecting the driver to go on his way. But, stubbornly, the driver stayed right where he was on his tail. Drago's face was beginning to throb now and harassment on the road was the last thing he needed. 'What do you want?' he muttered under his breath. 'If you think I'm a tourist with money, you're going to be sorely disappointed.'

He changed tactics, pressing the accelerator, intending to lose the person chasing him in that gutless old car. Surprisingly, it kept pace with him, tailgating and making him drive even faster. When they reached the top of the hill, beginning the steep descent, another vehicle coming towards them made

Drago swerve, losing control of the van entirely. In a panic, he wrenched at the wheel as it disobeyed him, seeming to have a mind of its own, lurching from side to side along the steep, winding road. Finally, it plunged through the flimsy barrier at the side of the road, rolling once before landing with a sickening crunch upside down on the rocks below. All this had taken place in less than ten minutes.

Bruno parked the battered car and crossed the road to look down at the smashed Winnebago, half expecting it to burst into flames but it didn't. He watched for a few moments to make sure there was no sign of life and then made a quick call from his mobile phone. By now other drivers had stopped, aware that something was wrong and assuming Bruno was summoning help. He was, in fact, reporting the success of his mission to Angelo. He shrugged, pulling a sad face at the people who had left their vehicles to stand as close to the cliff edge as they dared, peering down at the wreckage. Titillated and appalled by this scene of destruction and horror, nobody noticed when Bruno returned to his car and drove quietly away.

He didn't return it to the spacious garage at the villa where Angelo's well-polished silver limo resided, kept in tip-top condition by his chauffeur; questions would have been asked. Instead, he drove it across a field to a dilapidated hut that nobody used. That old car was not what it seemed. Beneath its battered exterior lay an engine capable of outrunning a police car and Bruno loved to drive it. Whistling happily, he concealed it under a dusty tarpaulin before making his way back to Angelo to report a mission completed without any mishaps.

★ ★ ★

Back at the villa, Rosalie didn't see Drago leave and wouldn't have cared if she had. Having run all around the gardens with Trizia, she'd worked up an appetite. Seated at the massive table in the warm heart of the villa's kitchen, she was drinking an ice cold strawberry milkshake, made with real berries and eating the most delicious chocolate cake she had ever tasted in her life.

6

Over the next few days, Angelo watched and waited, expecting Rosalie to mention her father and ask why he should leave so suddenly and without her but she never did. Instead, she accepted his decision to leave her behind at the villa, confirming Angelo's opinion that there had been no real affection between them. After all, what sort of father was Drago? A man willing to sacrifice his only child to serve his own needs.

Rosalie didn't associate any news of road accidents with her father. Such events were common enough everywhere — tourists driving too fast on those narrow cliff roads. And she was having too much fun in her grandfather's house and grounds to waste time watching television or paying any attention to broadcast news.

Known locally for his charitable works, no one was surprised when Angelo paid for the discreet funeral of one reported as an itinerant circus performer who had accidentally killed himself by driving off a cliff on the way to the ferry. The man's relatives who lived on a farm near Palestrina had made no response to the news of his death, showing no interest in either attending the man's funeral or contributing to its cost. And if Angelo's henchmen and servants knew the truth of the matter, they thought it best to keep quiet about it.

On the morning of the funeral, Angelo gave money to Rosalie and Trizia and sent them on an extended shopping expedition to make sure they didn't see or hear anything about it.

'We'll have a great time,' Trizia said, pink with pleasure at Angelo's generosity to herself as well as his granddaughter. 'I will show you the best boutiques with the finest clothes. I've never had the chance to buy anything there before.'

Although Trizia was a few years older, the two girls discovered they had a lot in common as they bonded over the shopping and Rosalie soon accepted the fact that she was here to stay. She belonged to her grandfather now and even began to think kindly of Drago for leaving her behind. She imagined him returning to Cleo and Cassia, boasting of a generous 'loan' from Angelo to revive the circus; she never thought for one moment that something bad might have happened to him.

Initially, she was shy in Angelo's presence, especially when they were alone, so he waited to gain her confidence before questioning her about her time with the circus and Drago, as well as her earlier days on her uncle's farm. He seemed hungry to know every detail of her life. Her answers were brief as she was still wary and not forthcoming but from the little she told him, he surmised that her early years with her mother and uncle had been a lot happier than the months she had spent with the circus troupe on the road. Eventually, punctuated by her tears, she told him what happened to Beppo and how she had lost Edmond, who had been her only friend. Young as she was, her world had been shaken by the loss of all the people she loved and her usual optimism had faltered; she no longer expected life to treat her well.

But Angelo was hugging a secret, keeping it close; he had already mapped out a brilliant future for her with the son of one of his oldest friends. It never occurred to him that Rosalie would be less than delighted to fall in with his plans.

Once more he sent her to town with Trizia, telling her to buy some more clothes — of real quality this time. He meant her to give the impression of being a lady, not a circus girl, and over the next few weeks, her confidence slowly returned. Aside from the time she had spent growing up with Uncle

Carlo and the horses, she had never been happier in her life.

Christmas was coming and when Angelo asked her what she would like for a present, she didn't need to think about it for a moment — she wanted a horse. This time, however, she was to be disappointed. Angelo was asthmatic as well as allergic to fur and couldn't tolerate any animals near him. Neither horses nor any other pets could be a part of her life. She accepted her grandfather's decision, grateful for the safe haven she had found in his home where she was treated like a princess.

She had a lovely room of her own, full of light from generously sized windows, two easy chairs, a luxurious king-sized bed with soft linen sheets and a walk-in wardrobe with space for many more clothes. Her favourite foods were always on hand, her clothes always freshly laundered and, for the first time in her life, she had more than one pair of shoes.

The only sour note was when Angelo asked her to go back to school, saying she needed to complete her education.

'You are not a peasant, child,' he said. 'But it concerns me that you can scarcely read or write.'

'I can, Grandpa. Enough to get by, anyway.'

'But I want you to do more than get by. You

should be capable of enjoying art and literature. And one day you'll marry and have a home of your own. If you can't read or keep proper accounts, your servants will find out and cheat you.'

'But I'm happy here, Grandpa, just as we are. I don't want to marry and leave you. Please don't make me do this. Don't send me back to school.'

'Then I suggest a compromise. If you won't go to school, we can have a private tutor come here. And as for marriage, well — we can talk about that later on. But you should know I have something in mind.'

Rosalie closed her eyes in relief, hearing only that she didn't have to go to school. She was looking forward to her sixteenth birthday, coming up in a couple of months, not realizing that her grandfather, who was unusually old-fashioned and set in his ways, considered sixteen a suitable age for a girl to be married.

The tutor turned out to be a pleasant surprise. A university student, supplementing his income by teaching Rosalie, he soon became her new best friend, although her grandfather insisted he should lodge elsewhere and report to the villa each day. The young man who had expected Rosalie to be the usual sulky, unwilling pupil, was pleased to find her intelligent and eager to learn. He was interested to hear that Edmond had been teaching her English before and was surprised to find how much she had already retained. She tried even harder to succeed at her lessons when she saw how her efforts impressed her grandfather.

And she had another interest, too, that she kept from her grandfather in case he didn't approve. After her disappointment over the horse, Trizia filled the gap by teaching her to ride her old Vespa, although they kept it a secret between them. As Rosalie had no licence, she had to be content with riding it around the grounds. Although it was no substitute for the joy of riding a horse, she hoped that eventually her grandfather would allow her the freedom of owning a scooter of her own.

Shortly after her birthday at the end of May, which the whole of Angelo's household celebrated in style, some visitors arrived at the villa. Rosalie knew they had to be important because of the frantic domestic refurbishing and cleaning that took place several weeks beforehand. They arrived in a black limousine, driven by a uniformed chauffeur and accompanied by a second car filled with armed 'minders'. These men didn't carry weapons in plain view but their suits were loose-fitting enough to conceal both holsters and guns, although Bruno kept his distance this time and didn't accost them.

Watching from her bedroom window, Rosalie saw this little convoy arrive and her heart sank. Sometimes her intuition was more of a curse than a blessing. The sun had gone in and she felt as if a cold wind was ushering in a black cloud; she didn't have a good feeling about these people.

Her grandfather welcomed them alone, sending an urgent message via Trizia that Rosalie was to dress in her finest clothes because he wanted her to impress his friends. She was to join them in the formal reception room in half an hour. As she put on a light, full-skirted floral dress that she hadn't yet worn, she tried to gain some impression of these visitors from Trizia but without success. The little maid just shrugged a shoulder and averted her eyes, refusing to be drawn. So, in spite of her misgivings, Rosalie went downstairs and entered the reception room, unsure what to expect.

The two old men were already smoking cigars and the room smelled of rich tobacco and several expensive male colognes.

'Ah, here she is. My little, new-found treasure.' Angelo greeted her arrival with a welcoming smile. 'Antonio — Francesco

— this is my lately discovered granddaughter, Rosalie. Drago's child.'

He pulled her towards him, putting an arm round her shoulders and hugging her although she could feel his tension which she found hard to comprehend. If her grandfather was the most powerful man in these parts, why did he need to create a good impression on these two? Their expensive Armani suits and gold jewellery couldn't hide the fact that they were brutish, coarse-featured men who wouldn't look out of place in a prison chain gang. And even though she herself had little experience of wealth, she felt sure they were displaying far too much gold for good taste.

'Rosalie, my love,' Angelo said. 'I'd like you to meet one of my oldest and dearest friends, Antonio Conti. And this is Francesco, his son.'

She murmured a pleasantry and tried to smile but felt her lips tremble instead. Antonio and his son had not yet spoken a word but, for some reason, they made her feel unreasonably afraid, as if she were in the presence of evil. They might be showing the outward trappings of civilization but she sensed it was only a social veneer and the calculating glint in Francesco's eyes made her shiver.

'Well, well.' Antonio cocked his head on one side, looking her over as if she were a horse he might buy. 'Not my idea of classical beauty but she's unusual and interesting enough with all that red-gold hair.' He turned back to Angelo. 'You're a dark horse, keeping this to yourself. And we haven't heard much of Drago lately. I always thought of him as your nephew — your sister's child. And when exactly did he marry? How come we never heard of it?'

'Oh, you know, families . . . ' Angelo laughed awkwardly, waving their queries away. 'His wife wasn't anyone special — a simple country girl.' The half-truths seemed to come easily to him. 'And he got her pregnant beforehand so nobody wanted a fuss. Drago kept the whole thing a secret for some time, thinking I wouldn't approve. Last year he came to see me, bringing this lovely child . . . '

'Oh? And where's Drago now? Still wasting his time with that futile circus of his?'

Angelo shrugged, ignoring the question. 'We're not here to talk about Drago. He's no longer a part of our lives. Antonio, please, accept my hospitality and stay with us for a while. Allow Rosalie and Francesco to get acquainted.'

Rosalie just managed to stop herself

128

gasping. Why should she want to spend time with a man twice her age and who had no more interest in her than she had in him? What could they possibly have in common?

Francesco glanced at his father and frowned. 'Bit busy at present,' he muttered. 'Got a lot on. Not sure we can spare the time.'

Rosalie breathed a silent sigh of relief. She didn't yet know what her grandfather had in mind but, with any luck, the black cloud hanging over them was about to be gone for good. Whatever mischief the old men were plotting, it was obvious that Francesco would stand firm in rejecting their plans.

'I'm sure there's nothing that cannot wait.' Antonio glared at his son. 'This matter needs to be settled and soon. Angelo and I have wanted an alliance between our two families for years and it's high time you married again — you grow sour without a woman in your life. Rosalie is suitable and young enough to be trained to our ways. And I want to hold at least one grandson in my arms before I die.'

'Yes, indeed. So do I.' Angelo nodded his approval, beaming.

Rosalie couldn't believe this was happening. That in this day and age she could be married off like a medieval bargaining chip to suit the needs of her grandfather. He was no better than Drago, after all; he had never really loved her and she had never been anything more than a pawn in his game. All her pleasure in her new lifestyle came crashing about her ears. This villa was far from being the safe haven she thought it to be. But even at this late stage she hoped to reason with her grandfather and divert him from this disastrous plan.

'Grandfather!' she whispered urgently, placing a hand on his arm. 'I need to speak to you now — alone.'

'Later, sweetheart,' he said, smiling and patting her hand as if indulging an imbecile. 'I know this must be a big surprise for you — '

'More like a shock.' She felt it was time for speaking the truth and she didn't try to keep her voice down or hide her contempt for Antonio and his son. 'I don't want to marry Francesco — any more than he wants to marry *me*. So you must excuse me, Grandfather, and entertain your visitors on your own. I'm going to my room.'

'Rosalie, stay!' Angelo snapped as if he were talking to a disobedient dog. 'You will not defy me.'

Rashly, she turned towards the door. Fast as a snake, Angelo seized her wrist and pulled her back to face him before giving her an open-handed slap across the face with the full force of his arm behind it. She reeled as the blow made her dizzy and that side of her face felt as if it were on fire — it was the same side that Drago had damaged before.

Sobbing, she wrenched herself free and ran from the room, scarcely able to see through her tears and with one eye already beginning to close. Was there no one in this world that she could believe in or trust? Angelo had proved to be just as treacherous and cruel as Drago. This was the first time she had defied him openly and retribution had been both painful and swift. She didn't know what the long-term consequences might be.

'A girl of spirit, at least.' She heard Antonio's mocking tone as she closed the door behind her. She would have to make plans and quickly. There was no one here she could trust — maybe not even Trizia.

★ ★ ★

As the afternoon wore on, she was surprised to be left alone. She heard footsteps on the stairs from time to time and braced herself for an imperious knock on the door from someone sent to bring her downstairs again, but none came. Her stomach growled with hunger as she had missed both lunch and

131

dinner but she didn't dare show her face. She had defied her grandfather and made him look foolish in front of his friends. He was a proud man and would find that hard to forgive. Her face throbbed but she didn't dare leave her room to go to the bathroom to bathe it. So she lay on her bed and closed her eyes, meaning only to rest for a moment but, because she was so exhausted, she fell into a deep and dreamless sleep.

★ ★ ★

Trizia knew something was wrong when Rosalie wasn't at lunch with Angelo and his visitors. Although the little maid waited on the family when they were dining alone, when there were visitors, Maria would usually call on a nephew of hers from the village. He had been a sous chef and was also used to waiting at tables. Today, however, he called in sick so most of his duties fell to Trizia. Already on edge, Maria had little patience with the girl and was missing the smooth cooperation she usually had from her nephew.

As Rosalie was still absent from the dinner table, Trizia assumed her friend was unwell and asked Maria if she had taken a tray up to her room.

'No, indeed. When would I have time to do

that? It's as much as I can do to prepare a gourmet meal without Dino to assist me. So will you stop your gab and deliver that zabaglione before it melts.'

'Well then, can I take her some?'

'No, you can't. Keep your mind on the job, Trizia. This is an important dinner party and I can't have you screwing things up. And when they're done with dessert, you can serve them coffee in the library.'

After the three men made themselves comfortable in the library, Trizia served coffee and petits fours, realizing that an atmosphere had developed between them. Antonio scowled at his son, more than a little displeased.

'What's wrong with the girl, son, that you take against her so?'

'Not now, Father — not while we're accepting Angelo's hospitality.'

Trizia knew they were speaking of Rosalie and started paying attention. People were often indiscreet in front of the servants, regarding them as largely invisible. But she knew she would learn more, if she were to serve the coffee quickly and leave the room. She left the door slightly ajar so that she could listen outside and hear what they said. With the meal satisfactorily over, Maria was unlikely to come in search of her now. Having spent the day standing up in the kitchen preparing food, the old woman would be taking a well-earned glass of wine and resting her swollen legs. Her husband would also be well into his cups by now.

Inside the library, the argument seemed to be escalating.

'Not good enough, Francesco.' Antonio was growing angry with his son.

'If you have an objection to Angelo's granddaughter, I want to hear of it now.'

Francesco sighed. 'All right. But don't say I didn't warn you. Rosalie is no more than a bastard, like her father before her.'

'What are you saying?' Antonio's expression grew thunderous.

'That Drago has never been married — to anyone. The girl is just the result of one of his casual affairs. And that's not all but I'd rather not go into it here.'

'You *will.*' Antonio glared at his son. 'I want to hear everything — now.'

'There have long been rumours that your friend Angelo slept with his sister and made her pregnant but nobody dared to say so. He has confirmed my suspicions today by calling Rosalie *granddaughter* — '

'Lies!' Angelo felt bound to interrupt. 'Filthy lies, put about by those who want to discredit me. Not that it's any of your business.'

'No? You made it my business when you asked me to marry that girl. I promise you, Father, it's true. Drago is Angelo's son — a child born of incest, palmed off on the circus owner.'

'And how come this is the first time I hear of this?' Antonio was shocked by this news. 'Why didn't you tell me before and save us a wasted journey?'

'Oh, I think you'll find it's not wasted. Think about it, Father. Angelo is supposed to be your best friend. When have we been summoned to a wedding celebration in this house? His own or that of any other family member? The answer is never. Because there haven't been any.'

'Insolent pup!' Angelo blustered, trying to turn the tables. 'And as for you, Antonio — you should make sure your own house is in order before you start throwing stones.' He stabbed a finger towards Francesco. 'What about *your* boy's mother? Yes, you married her — more fool you. A table dancer who took off her clothes for the amusement of men and who died young from some unspecified social disease — '

'Don't you dare put forward such scandalous rumours!' Antonio was breathing heavily now, shocked at the turn the conversation was taking. 'My wife was an angel — a saint. I would kill you with my bare hands before I let you speak ill of her — '

Realizing these men were far too involved in their argument to notice her, Trizia moved forward to watch them through the crack in the door. She saw Angelo lunge towards his desk, intending to pick up a candlestick or an ink well for use as a weapon but Francesco was younger and moved a lot faster. Producing a knife from somewhere near his ankle and with an expertise born of experience, he slashed Angelo quickly and deeply across the throat and jumped back to avoid the resultant cascade of blood from soiling his clothes. Already dead before falling face down across his desk, Angelo's body convulsed and quickly bled out.

Outside, Trizia clapped her hands over her mouth to suppress a scream. If she were discovered as a witness to what had just happened, her own death would swiftly follow.

'That was — a little impulsive,' Antonio said, grimacing at the still-twitching body of his one-time friend. 'Are you sure we're quite ready to take over his empire?'

'More than ready.' Francesco smiled, wiping his knife on a handkerchief before returning it to its scabbard and showing no remorse for what he'd just done. 'We need only to ensure the loyalty of Angelo's men. Those who don't care to embrace our cause can join him in paradise instead.'

'What of the girl? She's a liability. It could be safest to leave her here.'

'Heavens, no. She's worth money. I'll take her down to the docks in the morning. I know someone who makes a good business out of selling young girls — especially *virgo intacta.*'

'I have taught you well, son. You think of everything,' Antonio applauded softly.

Trizia backed away and moved quickly and quietly away from the hall, wanting to hear no more.

★   ★   ★

Rosalie was rudely shaken awake to find the room in darkness and Trizia leaning over her bed, carrying a torch. She seemed agitated.

'Wha-whassamatter?' she said, blinking as she tried to return from the depths of sleep.

'Ssh!' Trizia whispered urgently. 'It's the middle of the night so keep your voice down and pay attention to what I say. Your grandfather is dead. Those Conti people have murdered him.'

'What?' Rosalie blinked again, finding it hard to take in this news. 'Why? Not because of me? Because I refused to marry his friend's son?'

'Oh, there's a lot more to it than that. There was a huge argument and they were all too angry to keep quiet. So I listened outside the door to hear what they had to say. That Francesco is a piece of work. He's been urging his father to take Angelo's place for years while the old men preferred to keep the alliance and remain friends. But Francesco was suspicious of your sudden arrival in Angelo's life. He found out the truth about you and your father and waited for just the right moment to reveal it. When the master turned his back for a moment, going to his desk for a weapon, Francesco produced a knife and slashed his throat.'

'Ohh!' Rosalie closed her eyes, finding it all too easy to picture the scene. 'But where was Bruno? He always took such good care of Grandfather.'

'Drugged.' Trizia sighed. 'Along with Maria. Must have been in the wine they shared after dinner. Matteo was already on board with the new regime. And now they're all downstairs in the kitchen, sampling the master's best wines. I overheard them laughing and saying they're coming for you in the morning.'

'What for? Francesco can't possibly want

to marry me now.'

'Oh, he never intended to. He has a friend down at the marina. A man who's always looking for girls to sell to rich men with yachts — especially if they're still virgins like you.'

Rosalie clapped her hand to her mouth, suddenly aware of the danger she faced.

'So now you see why you need to get out of here well before daybreak,' Trizia said. 'You can take my scooter.'

'That's right. We can both go.'

'No. My scooter's not strong and two girls are more likely to get caught than one. You can wear my jacket and take a scarf to wrap round your head. The gatekeeper's half asleep at this time of night. Give a cheery wave and he'll think that it's me.'

'This isn't a good plan, Trizia. I don't like leaving you here. They could punish you when they find out you let me go.'

'Not if I curse you and say you stole my old scooter. It's insured so I don't care if you drop it in the sea when you've finished with it. I'll get a new one.'

'Trizia, are you quite sure my grandfather's dead? He might still be alive.'

'Go and see for yourself, if you must. But Francesco is nothing if not thorough.' Trizia gave a small shudder and drew a finger across her throat. 'The master is still where they left him — lying across his desk. There's a lot of blood — and a very bad smell.' She drew herself up as if pulling herself together. 'You don't need to see that. Keep your memory of your grandfather as he was.'

'But — '

'We're wasting time. You need to be far away from here before they come looking for you. Right now they're celebrating — drinking themselves into the ground with the best wines from your grandfather's cellar. With any luck, they'll fall asleep and won't find out you're gone till the morning.'

'But Trizia, I have no money. I won't get very far without that.'

'The master keeps a lot of money in his desk but the drawer's locked and he's lying right over it. But sometimes he forgets and leaves money in the pockets of his suits. A valet got punished last year for robbing him.'

'Small change? Not enough to finance a journey.'

'You think?' Trizia smiled. 'Small change to your grandfather but a small fortune to us. Let's go and have a look while everyone's down there drinking themselves senseless.'

Rosalie sighed. 'Until today they were all my grandfather's men. They don't show much loyalty, do they?'

Trizia shrugged. 'They have no choice. That's how things are in this part of the world. They have to change their loyalties and acknowledge Conti as the new boss, if they wish to survive. He doesn't ask for allegiance — he demands it. Those who refuse don't last long. Antonio is the big man now so they're all down there, swearing fealty and hanging on his every word.'

While they were still upstairs, they went into Angelo's suite and no one was there to stop them going through his unlocked wardrobe and searching the pockets of his clothes. Trizia was right. Three of his jackets contained quite large sums of money — more than enough to send Rosalie safely on her way.

In constant fear of discovery and holding hands tightly to stop themselves shaking, the two girls crept down the servants' stairs towards the back door. They could hear Antonio still holding forth, cracking jokes in the kitchen and laughing. Rosalie wondered how he could do that with the man he had called his best friend lying upstairs at his desk in a pool of his own blood.

After making sure the coast was clear, the two girls closed the back door softly behind them and made their way to the shed where Trizia kept her only means of transport. It wasn't impressive — a faded blue scooter that had travelled many kilometres already — but to Rosalie it meant the difference between freedom and a life of slavery. She made one last attempt to get Trizia to leave with her.

'Look, there's no one about,' she said. 'So why not come with me? They won't find out we're gone till the morning.'

'There's still the gatekeeper and he'll be well in Antonio's camp by now, if he knows what's good for him. Two girls wobbling along on that thing will raise his suspicions. Rosalie, I'll be OK. Don't worry about me. I'll pack up right now and go to my aunt in the village — she'll look after me.'

Not wanting to announce their departure by starting the scooter too soon and making a noise, the two girls wheeled it until all that remained between Rosalie and freedom was the front gate itself.

'Go to one of the smaller ferries,' Trizia advised. 'They'll expect you to choose one of the big ones because they're more frequent. I just hope you can get away from the island before they come after you.'

'Thank you for everything.' Rosalie hugged her diminutive friend. 'If it weren't for you and your kindness, I'd have slept until morning and it would have been too late.'

'What are friends for?' Trizia returned the

embrace. 'We'll meet again soon, I'm sure, and then we'll laugh about this adventure.'

Rosalie tried to smile but she couldn't. Trizia's words sounded hollow somehow.

'Ride confidently.' Trizia made a shooing motion with her hands. 'And don't forget to wave to the gatekeeper. I always do.'

'OK,' Rosalie said, not trusting herself to say more as she was in danger of bursting into tears, overcome by her friend's kindness. Fortunately, she knew how to ride the scooter but now she would have to put that learning to the test.

She turned the key and the little engine responded immediately. Trizia's boyfriend was a mechanic and he kept it well tuned. She wound the girl's distinctive red scarf around her head to hide her bruised face and drove towards the gate, honking imperiously.

'All right. All right, you foxy little bitch,' the gatekeeper grumbled, rousing himself from his boozy slumbers to open the gate sufficiently to let her pass. 'Got the hots again, have you? Mustn't keep the boyfriend waiting.' And he gave a mocking bow as Rosalie drove through, trying not to wobble as she steered past him. It was tricky but she managed the cheery wave.

Still fearing to hear the sound of that sleek black limo coming after her, she followed the tortuous track leading down from the mountain as the sun rose. Soon she found herself on the main road leading to the various ferries. Riding as fast as she dared, with the wind pulling the red scarf like a plume behind her, she didn't look back as she headed for freedom and whatever the rest of her life might hold.

7

Leo glowered across the small patch of water separating him from the mainland, anxious to get away from Sicily just as soon as he could. His attempt to visit his Italian relatives had been a complete disaster and he needed to banish it from his thoughts and get on with his life.

Although it was early, the sun was already up in a cloudless blue sky, making it too hot to wait in the car. He climbed out and leaned against it instead, lighting a cigarette. What a fool he had been to come here. Dante, his father, had always advised against making any contact with their Sicilian relatives. In fact, his father never talked about them at all except to say that there had been some family drama and that Leo's grandfather had sent Dante to Australia, warning him never to return.

It had been good advice. Only now was Leo beginning to realize that by trying to fill in the gaps in his family history, he had stirred up a hornets' nest. As an easy-going Australian with no real enemies of his own, he had found it hard to believe that old grudges could remain alive and just as poisonous after so many years.

Although the surname Marino was common enough, it had been surprisingly easy to trace his father's relatives who remained living in or near Messina, especially as his father's older brother Alberto was still alive. Too late, he realized he should have tested the temperature of his relatives' feelings before turning up on their doorstep unannounced. Unfortunately, it had been Alberto himself who answered his knock at the door. Although his uncle struck him as a much older man, he bore such a striking resemblance to his own father, Dante, that Leo was momentarily overcome by emotion, unable to speak. But there the similarities ended. While the lines on his father's face had come from good humour and laughter, his uncle's features bore only the deep crevices of discontent. He kept Leo standing on the doorstep, speaking in broken English and refusing to let him exercise his own faltering Italian.

'You say you my nephew? Big deal as they say in American movie. You expect us to roll out red carpet? Why you come here? To show us peasants how Dante make better life for himself in Australia with the money he steal from me?'

'That is a lie.' Leo felt bound to defend the father he had loved. 'Dante Marino was always an honest and honourable man until the day he died. He would never cheat or steal from anyone, let alone family.'

'So you come to tell me Dante is dead? *Bene*. I hope he roast in hell now.' Working himself into a rage Alberto beat himself on the chest. 'I — I am eldest son. When our father die, it is tradition our vineyard should come to me. But no. The old man sick and losing his mind — he sell out to his cousin.' Alberto's voice rose as his anger increased. 'Then Dante take all the money an' run off to Australia. Me an' my family have nothing. Life is difficult here for a very long time.'

'I'm sorry. I didn't know.' At the same time Leo felt certain this wasn't the whole story. There had to be a lot more to it than his uncle said.

'*Si*. Dante turn his back on us — leave us in hardship — while you get a stable filled with fine horses. Is that right? Is it fair? Don' look so surprised. We have internet, same as you. Simpler to keep an eye on people these days.'

That sounded menacing enough for Leo to feel uneasy. Only now did he realize what a mistake it had been to come here, digging up old bones.

'You go now.' The old man smiled but there was no kindness in it. 'Thank you for coming to tell me Dante is dead. I wish only that I could dance on his grave. Go now an' don' trouble comin' back. An', as they say in American film — watch you back.'

'Oh?' Leo felt a renewed flicker of irritation. 'Are you threatening me?'

His uncle's smile became sly. 'An' we have another saying. Revenge is a dish best eaten cold.'

With that, he slammed the front door in Leo's face. Leo had been given no chance to meet any other members of the family. He had seen two women peeping at him from a doorway in the hall but they looked too scared to argue with his uncle and invite him in. It was a hot day and he was sweating profusely, even in his lightweight suit, and although he had travelled for hours, taking the ferry to come over and see them, he hadn't been offered so much as a glass of water from his uncle's house. The suit had been a mistake — he could see that now. He would have done better to arrive casually dressed in his usual T-shirt and jeans.

Driving to the ferry and going back over that brief conversation, he was beginning to wish he'd stayed at home. Not that he had expected a royal welcome from his father's

Italian relatives but the bitterness of the encounter with Alberto had been a rude awakening. After acquainting himself with the Italian side of his family, he had hoped to take a leisurely drive across Italy, exploring the country of his father's birth. But he didn't feel like doing that now. He hadn't known what to expect from his father's brother but certainly not so much venom and condemnation. Obviously, these old wounds were far from healed and the family feud was still very much alive.

He sighed, wishing the ferry was on its way. He already had a return ticket to the mainland, choosing to go with one of the smaller lines rather than the state ferry which was often delayed while it waited for trains.

This was his first trip overseas as he had never been one for travelling when he was young; there had always been too much to do, especially in a small hands-on stable like their own. Sometimes it seemed as if people who looked after race-horses never slept. But it was a discipline he was used to, having grown up with it. The horses always came first. Dante and his partner, Jim Halloran, had trained several champions and were successful enough to afford a few good horses of their own. His father had often told him the story of their friendship, struck up on the month-long sea voyage to Australia and of meeting and falling in love with Jim's sister, Maureen, who had become his mother.

Sadly, Jim Halloran had been killed in a car accident just a few years into their partnership but Dante and his wife, Maureen, had enjoyed many years of happy marriage before they both died of strokes within months of each other, leaving their only son bereft. They had been such a happy family together.

Being left to rattle around in their big house alone had inspired Leo to take the first real holiday he'd taken in the whole of his life, deciding to visit Italy in the hope of finding some of their long-lost relatives, wanting to meet the people who had known his father as a young man only to discover it had been a foolish notion. With the trip soured, he couldn't wait to get back to Australia.

Looking around, he noticed that he wasn't the only one waiting impatiently for the ferry. A young girl, with untidy, tangled red hair was sitting astride a scooter, also watching the ferry that hadn't yet started to cross the small expanse of water between here and the mainland. Vibrating with tension, she was muttering to herself, almost praying for it to set off. Her fair skin was freckled by the sun and the smell of fear surrounded her, mingling with her sweat. He had her pegged as a runaway for sure, forever glancing at the road behind them as if she expected wild horsemen to come galloping after her. She closed her eyes occasionally, taking deep breaths to steady herself, doing her best to stay calm.

As more vehicles piled up alongside and behind them, waiting to board the ferry which seemed at last to be on its way towards them, the vessel looming closer every minute, he realized she was hunkering down beside his vehicle, making herself and her scooter as small and inconspicuous as possible. Then he saw that she was crying softly, too, the tears rolling down her face as, impatiently, she scrubbed them away with her fingers.

Having already blundered into enough trouble on his own account today, Leo knew he should ignore her and not interfere but he couldn't bear the sight of a young girl so obviously in distress. She probably didn't speak English, either, but he decided to try that first.

'I can see you're upset, miss,' he said. 'Do you need any help?'

'Not unless you can make me invisible,' she whispered back in English, confirming that she understood.

'Are you running away from home? You

should think it over carefully before you do. Your family will be worried.'

She looked at him properly then before giving a bitter little laugh and shaking her head.

'You are kind, signor, but you don't unnerstand. Jus' ignore me an' leave me alone.'

Leo wanted to do just that but his 'white knight' instinct had already kicked in. He couldn't turn away and leave such a fragile young girl to the mercy of someone cruel enough to bruise her face so severely. That alone was testimony to the ill treatment she had received. He reasoned that she must have some purpose in making this crossing other than casting herself into the unknown. All he had to do was take her with him and deliver her safely to the people who must be waiting for her on the other side. It would be his good deed for the day and he needed to feel good about himself after the poor welcome he had received at his uncle's home.

'OK,' he said. 'Help me lift your scooter into the trunk of the car. It's not going to fit but we can cover it with a rug to disguise it.'

Rosalie needed no second invitation. She had looked into the face of this stranger — an American, she thought — and decided he was to be trusted. Leo in turn was surprised to find she was stronger than she looked and more than capable of helping him wrestle the scooter into the trunk of the car. Of course the lid wouldn't close but with Leo's luggage around it the scooter was largely concealed, and she knew Francesco and his hirelings wouldn't expect to see her travelling in the company of such a well-dressed tourist.

Without waiting to be invited, she jumped into the back seat of the car and covered herself with a rug she found there.

'What are you doing?' Leo said. 'You'll suffocate in this weather.'

'Better to die than be sold as a slave to some rich man on a yacht.'

Leo looked at her and was tempted to laugh at this piece of melodrama until he realized she was genuinely scared.

She had concealed herself not a moment too soon. Causing angry shouts from the people already waiting beside their cars, a sleek black limo arrived to join the people waiting to board the ferry. The driver pressed it forward past everyone to park with a squeal of brakes in the dirt on the side of the road, raising a cloud of dust as he did so. It was amazing that he hadn't side-swiped any other cars.

'Look at that! I hate people queue-barging!' Bristling with anger, an elderly

English tourist left his vehicle to confront the middle-aged Italian who climbed out of the limo. The newcomer looked the tourist up and down and ignored him as if he hadn't spoken at all.

'Hey, you! I'm speaking to you!' the old man persisted, having no sense of danger as he continued to accost the driver of the limo. He jumped back at once when the Italian hissed at him like a snake and brandished a wicked-looking knife. Thoroughly alarmed, the tourist retreated to the safety of his own vehicle as fast as his arthritic legs could carry him.

The newcomer put the knife away and started looking around as if searching for someone. Two other men climbed out of the vehicle and joined the search. They were efficient and thorough, even peering into some of the cars. Leo drummed his fingers on the wheel, trying to look bored and nonchalant. Some minutes later, without finding their quarry, the men regrouped, shrugging and shaking their heads.

Although his Italian left a lot to be desired, Leo knew enough to make sense of what they were saying, picking up the words 'not here' and 'gone another way'. He was relieved that they had scarcely glanced at his car. He didn't fancy tangling with people who looked like gangsters and carried knives.

'Hurry!' he heard their leader say in Italian. 'Go to the other ferry. We must catch her and bring her back to Francesco before she reaches the mainland.'

The men climbed back into the limo and began to reverse away from the scene, causing even more dust and inconvenience than before, just as the ferry arrived. The doors opened and the arriving vehicles streamed out. Soon, Leo, who was almost at the head of the queue, took a place at the front. He would be one of the first to disembark when they reached the mainland.

In the back of the car, still under the rug in the dark, Rosalie gave a long sigh and started to breathe again, feeling weak with relief. Somehow, against all odds, she had made her escape. Her troubles were by no means over but, for now at least, she was free.

They reached the mainland without incident. Leo drove off the ferry and found somewhere to park nearby. After making sure no one was watching, he hauled the girl out of the car and stood glancing around.

'There you are, then,' he said. 'Safe on the mainland. Will someone be here to meet you and take you home?'

She took a step away from him, staring at him as if he had betrayed her. 'No! You said you would help me. You can't give me up to them now.'

'Not to the people who hurt you, no.' He made a placating gesture with both hands. 'I thought . . . surely there has to be somebody coming to meet you?'

She shook her head. 'No. Is OK. Jus' give me scooter an' I go. I thank you for you kindness but now I mus' go.'

'But I can't let you leave. Not like this. You haven't even told me your name.'

'Is Rosalie. Please, sir, give me bike an' I go.'

'Well, Rosalie, I think you need to tell me the whole story. All of it. You owe me that much at least.'

'I owe? You mean I owe you for ride in you car?' She pulled a wad of notes from the pocket of her jeans.

'God, no. That's not what I meant. And that's a lot of money you have there. Put it away before somebody sees it.'

She shrugged and thrust it back into the pocket of her jeans. 'Sir, jus' give me the bike an' I go.' She kept glancing back towards the small stretch of water as if she were still afraid of pursuit.

'No. Get back in the car — the front seat beside me, this time. We'll find a café where we can have breakfast. You need to tell me exactly what's going on in your life.'

She stared at him, still unsure what to do. This American was old, of course. He had to be well over thirty but he did have really kind eyes. Dark-haired, he was good-looking and sexy, too, although he didn't seem too aware of that. She felt herself blushing, hoping that he couldn't read her mind.

'Rosalie, you can trust me,' he said, cutting across her thoughts. 'You do know you have nothing to fear from me.'

'I suppose,' she said, knowing she sounded less than gracious while she made up her mind what to do. If she were to set off alone on the scooter, she would be clearly visible on the main road; Francesco and his minions would capture her easily and she'd rather not think of what might happen after that. For now, it seemed better to take her chances with this new friend.

Her rescuer, after pausing briefly at a service station to fill up his car and buy a cool drink for each of them, put a good few kilometres on the clock before finding a cheerful café in a small village where he ordered the promised breakfast. This turned out to be antipasto and early lunch.

Having had little to eat the previous day, Rosalie found she was starving. She ate without inhibition, feasting on the freshly baked bread, sardines and various vegetables pickled in oil, accompanied by several cups of good, strong coffee. He let her eat and didn't ask any questions until she sat back with a gentle belch to show she was replete.

'Now then,' he said, holding out his hand to make a formal introduction. 'I am Leo Marino. And you are Rosalie . . . ?'

'Marino? But that's an Italian name,' she interrupted him, surprised. 'I thought you American.'

'*Si*. A lot of people make that mistake when I'm travelling in Europe. I am in fact an Australian.'

'Australian? Really? I never met an Australian before.'

'No? There are many Australians born of Italian parents.' Almost ready to embark on his own life history, he realized she was diverting attention away from herself. 'But we're not here to talk about me. I need to know what's going on in your life.'

'What's to know?' She shrugged and looked down at her empty plate, avoiding his gaze. 'I just a girl. Only sixteen.'

'Yes but if I'm going to help you, I need to know what I'm getting into here.' He peered at her injured face. 'For starters, who did that to your face? And what did you do to deserve it?'

'It was my grandfather. He want me to marry this man. He get very angry when I refuse.'

'And your parents. What did they have to say about that?'

Rosalie shrugged. 'My mother is dead and my father is gone. Those men killed my grandfather — the ones who were chasing me. That's why I had to run away.'

'OK. Wind it back a moment. I'm trying to decide what's the truth or if you're a very inventive liar. And what was that crazy story about being sold into slavery?'

'Oh, I wish it was only a story — but it's not. There are rich men with yachts down at the marina — they think money can buy anything and don't care about breaking the law. They pay good money for young girls like me who haven't been touched.'

'I can't believe this. It's like a story from the *Arabian Nights*.'

'OK.' Angered, Rosalie rose to her feet. 'Believe what you like. I don' care. Thanks for your help an' for feeding me, sir. Now give me bike an' I go.'

'You stay right where you are.' Serious now, he glared at her until she dropped back into her seat. 'Now, stop lying and tell me the real story behind all this. I think you're running away and you stole that bike as well as the money.'

'No. The money was in my grandfather's clothes. He doesn't need it now because he's dead.' Feeling betrayed by the old man, she found it hard to be sorry he was gone. 'The scooter was a gift from a friend.'

'Go on.'

Over more coffee, accompanied by a large brandy for Leo, she told him the whole sorry tale in detail. When she was finished, he blew out a long breath.

'So. You believe me now?' she asked in a small voice.

'I suppose I have to,' he said. 'But Rosalie, we still have a problem. You're only sixteen. A minor in the eyes of the law — '

'What is minor?'

'You have to be eighteen years old to be a free agent and do as you please — an adult.'

'Oh, that's easy. I can be eighteen if you like,' she said breezily. 'I'm tall for my age an' I have no papers jus' now so nobody know.'

'Christ.' He swore softly. 'No ID, no papers and no passport, I suppose?'

'What is . . . ?' She frowned, looking puzzled.

'You don't even know what that is? Hell.' He swore again and groaned. 'What on earth am I to do with you, Rosalie?'

'Like I say. Don' worry 'bout me.' Bravely,

she tried to smile. 'I'll be OK. I have lots of money and bike — '

'Uh-uh. The bike can easily be traced back to you. If you're coming with me, we'll need to leave it behind.'

She brightened immediately. 'So you take me with you? I go to Australia?'

'Whoa! Don't get carried away here. Rosalie, think. Surely, there's someone here in Italy who can take proper care of you?'

Slowly, she opened her eyes wide and shrugged expressively, shaking her head.

8

It took Leo some time to realize what he had got himself into. Rosalie trusted him completely, expecting him to find a way out of her dilemma. At first he had been inclined to take some of her tales with a pinch of salt but by now he was convinced that her life might well be in danger if he left her to fall into the hands of Francesco and his gang of ruffians. It had been his intention to get back to Rome as quickly as possible and take the first available flight to Australia. That was all but impossible now. In addition, although she was sixteen, Rosalie wasn't like any of the modern teenagers he knew. Reticent as she was to talk about herself at first, when he did manage to get her to open up, he gathered that she had led a sheltered life on her uncle's farm in Umbria before joining her father's travelling circus. After that, she ended up in the care of a grandfather whose wealth seemed to come from questionable sources. She seemed like someone from a bygone era, having no idea how the modern world worked.

After an early evening meal at a café, he did

his best to explain the situation in simple terms.

'Rosalie, listen to me. Without a passport, I can't even hire a room for you to spend the night in a hotel.'

'OK.' She gave him a sunny smile. 'I sleep in your car. Is enough room for me.'

'It isn't just a question of size. At the hotel, I'll have to register. People will take my car away and put it in a garage. They won't expect to find a girl sleeping inside it.'

'OK.' She came back to the same old argument. 'Jus' give me bike an' let me go. I don' want to be trouble for you. I thank you, Leo — you've done more than enough and I'll be OK now. I disappear — maybe pretend to read cards for tourists. Maybe hitch up with some more circus people — '

'Yes and how long will it be before you run into Francesco or his father? You almost certainly will. What happens then?'

'I don' know.' She shrugged, looking miserable.

'And I need to go home soon. I have a successful racing stables and good people working for me. But no real decisions can be made while I'm away. That's always down to me.'

'You have racing stables? Horses? Well, why didn't you say so before?' Her face lit up with enthusiasm once again. 'My uncle raised me around horses. Do you keep many?'

'Not really. It isn't a huge concern. Just a dozen or so in training for other people and a few of my own. When my father first came to Australia, he bought the stables jointly with Jim Halloran, a guy he met on the ship coming out. They had so much in common they became best friends. Then my father fell in love with Jim's sister, Maureen, who was my mother. They appeared to be set for life but, unfortunately, my own parents died only recently within months of each other.'

'That would have been hard.' Rosalie bit her lip in sympathy, thinking how bereft she had felt when she lost Uncle Carlo.

'Uhuh.' Leo felt his throat tighten with unexpected emotion. He didn't want to break down in front of the girl so he cleared it instead. 'That's why I wanted to come to Sicily — to see if I had any relatives left. To cut a long story short, the visit wasn't a success.'

'People can be suspicious of strangers.' Rosalie was thinking of the many towns and villages where the circus hadn't been welcome. 'But Leo, I'm good with horses. No — better than good — I am expert! Maybe I come to Australia now an' I work for you.'

164

'Whoa, I don't think so, Rosalie. It isn't that easy. There's a lot of red tape to get through first. You're a young person with no papers. No passport. And it's impossible for anyone to travel without one.'

'You say this because you don' wan' me to come to Australia.' She folded her arms and her mouth settled in a sulky line.

'Rosalie, it isn't a question of what I want. Or you for that matter. I could be accused of kidnapping you.'

'Who's left to accuse you?' She gave an expressive shrug. 'My father is long gone and my grandfather's dead.'

'You still can't go anywhere without a valid passport.'

'So, I mus' get one,' she muttered, looking speculatively at a tourist's shoulder bag. 'You say I can come to Australia if I have this passport?'

Leo followed the direction of her gaze. 'Not just any passport — you can't steal someone else's. A passport is a means of identity, relating only to you. To live and work in Australia, you must be a citizen. So it has to be an Australian passport, too.'

'But you would take me with you? Yes? If only I had an Australian passport?'

'And you don't. So it's no good discussing it further because the whole idea's crazy.'

'Sure. It went crazy as soon as you helped me escape from Francesco.'

'Right. I'm not usually that impulsive.' He sat back, regarding her, thinking for a moment. 'Look, I have an old school friend at the Australian Embassy in Rome. He might be able to offer us some advice.'

'We go to Rome?' She grinned at him, eyes sparkling and softly clapping her hands. 'I love to see Rome. Francesco and his father won't go there. Too many police, too many . . . ' She paused, searching for the word. 'Officials.'

'That's the first good news I've heard. But first, we have to leave the scooter behind.'

Reluctantly, Rosalie helped him wrestle the Vespa out of his car and parked it some distance away under the trees. She sighed and patted the saddle, seeing it as the final loss of her independence. Without it, she was totally reliant upon Leo and what he may or may not be able to do for her.

They made good time, driving long hours to get back to Rome as quickly as possible. Leo bought pillows so that they could sleep in the car although Rosalie, stretching out on the back seat, was more comfortable than he was himself, dozing fitfully in cramped conditions in the front seat. He thought with longing of air-conditioned hotels and clean linen sheets on a well-made bed. Why was he doing this? What was making him give up so much for this little waif?

The next day, to his profound relief, they arrived in Rome.

Rosalie, relaxed and happy now her face had subsided and her pursuers were left far behind, was taking in all the sights like a tourist, gasping with wonder at the Coliseum, the many squares with their cafés and tourists, the Bernini fountains. Leo could think of nothing but calling on Harry Wilson at the Australian Embassy, hoping his old friend would find a solution without straining the friendship.

Once there, he insisted on leaving Rosalie behind in the embassy gardens although she wanted to accompany him and go inside.

'You've gone to so much trouble because of me. I should be there to see what he say.'

'I'm afraid I know what he'll say,' Leo said. 'I just don't want you to hear it.'

'You think your friend won' like me?'

'It isn't a question of liking, Rosalie. He'll be a lot more honest with me if you aren't there.'

Much as he expected, Harry was far from impressed. A conventional civil service type with a neat haircut and wearing a spotless cream linen suit, he greeted Leo with a slap on the back and a jovial prod in the ribs.

'What brings you here, mate? Lost your passport? Always happening. Blame the government for making the damned things so small.' His smile quickly faded when Leo explained what had happened to Rosalie and the real purpose of his visit.

'Whew! Doesn't sound like old sober-sides, Leo. Never knew you were one for taking such risks. First you abduct a young girl from under the nose of the Sicilian Mafia and now you expect me to wave a magic wand and get her a passport.'

'I don't expect anything, Harry. I'm just hoping you can advise me — tell me what to do.'

'What you should do is forget the whole thing. At least half of her tales will be lies, anyway. Think about it — circus people, feuding Mafia barons and murderous gangsters. No. You need to get yourself on the first plane out of here and leave the kid far behind.'

'No, Harry, that isn't an option. It's gone too far now and I'm too deeply involved. I have to help her.'

Harry walked to the window and stared down at Rosalie, who was kneeling beside the ornamental fish pond, looking at her reflection and trailing her fingers in the water.

'Is that her? The lanky redhead? Down there by the pond?'

'Yeah.' Leo followed his friend's gaze and let go a sigh.

'All right, Leo, what's the deal? You think you're in love with her or what?'

'God, no! Look again, Harry. She's just a child — a lost child.'

'And that's exactly what she wants you to think — to make you responsible. With respect, Leo, you don't know this country but I've lived here for some time and I do. Rome is full of kids just like this one. Kids living like gypsies and preying on tourists. It's a wonder she hasn't taken you into some dark alley where her boyfriend is waiting to rob you. And don't try to tell me she wouldn't.'

'She's not like that. D'you really think me such a poor judge of character?'

'Not at all. But I do think she's taking advantage of your soft heart. She'll string you along until one day you trust her with a large sum of money and then — poof! She'll vanish into thin air.' And Harry laughed, expecting Leo to join him. He didn't.

'I'd better leave,' he said instead. 'I didn't come here to ask the impossible or to embarrass you — although it seems that I have.'

'No, Leo, I'm sorry — I didn't mean to upset you. Sometimes I can be a clumsy oaf.'

169

At last Harry realized his teasing was inappropriate. 'You wouldn't have come to see me at all unless you were desperate.'

'That's true. But one of those bastards had beaten her up, Harry. You should have seen her face.'

Harry went back to his desk, found a notepad and started scribbling.

'I can't help you myself,' he said. 'Got too much to lose — my job, my pension, maybe even my wife. She loves the life here in Rome and she'll kill me if I do something stupid and we have to leave. Don't ask me how but I know of this guy who's very good with fake passports — especially Australian. I've sent him one or two people before.'

Leo glanced at what Harry had written. 'Delbert Cromwell?' He grinned.

'Sounds like someone out of a Victorian melodrama.'

Harry ignored the remark. 'You'll laugh on the other side of your face when you hear how much he charges. His illegal services don't come cheap.' He no longer seemed to find the situation amusing. 'And by the way, I'd rather you didn't mention that the recommendation came from me.'

'Oh? Then how shall I . . . ?'

'I leave that to your ingenuity. I can't afford to let someone like Cromwell get any sort of hold over me. Who knows where it would end?' Harry muttered, going to the window to take another look at Rosalie. 'And give my regards to your pretty little friend.'

Leo shook hands with Harry to say farewell and found himself pulled into a bear hug as they reached the door.

'You old dog, you! Who would have thought it,' Harry said, smiling and shaking his head.

Leo now realized his reputation was shot. Clearly, Harry didn't believe a word he'd been saying about his relationship with the girl. Unwittingly, Rosalie herself confirmed it by hurling herself at him as if they had been parted for days instead of less than an hour and planting a moist kiss on his cheek.

'What a lovely garden,' she sighed with contentment. 'I had such a good time, talking to the fish. How'd it go, then? You have my passport?'

'No, I don't, minx. There's a lot more to it than that. We have to see a man called Delbert Cromwell. And it will probably cost us an arm and a leg.'

★ ★ ★

Delbert Cromwell was a fellow Australian; a small, weaselly little man with faded red hair and a matching ginger moustache. He worked from a small, stifling office situated in a tiny back street behind a small delicatessen. It reeked of the hams and sausages stored in the room next door. There was no air-conditioning, not even a fan.

He glanced at the note that Harry had scribbled, clearly not deceived as to its origins, turning it over in his hands and all but sniffing it.

'Nice quality paper. Embassy paper if I don't miss my guess.' He spoke with a strong Australian accent. 'Well, it'll cost you, mate,' he said without any attempt to soften the blow. 'Is it just the one passport or two?'

'Just for Rosalie here.'

'Rosalie. Pretty name. What's the other one?'

'Other one?' Rosalie blinked at him, making him roll his eyes.

'Your surname, of course. You can use any surname you want.'

'Oh?' Rosalie considered this, hoping to dream up something exotic.

'Make it Marino,' Leo said. 'Cause a lot less trouble if it's the same as mine — we can say she's a relative. Make it a lot easier when we get home, too.'

'OK.' Delbert held out his hand for Leo's passport. 'Lend me yours and I'll make sure all the dates correspond.'

'Really?' Leo hesitated, unwilling to surrender his passport to this seedy little man.

'And that'll be . . . ' The man made a quick calculation, head on one side. 'Three thousand Australian dollars, please.'

'Three thousand dollars?' Leo stared at him. 'But that's outrageous.'

'Take it or leave it.' Delbert sat back and looked up at him. 'I'm running a risk doing this sort of business at all. Go to jail for a long time if I'm caught. So would she.' He jerked his chin towards Rosalie.

'And do your forgeries pass muster? Ever had any trouble before?' Leo wanted to make quite sure before he parted with either his passport or any money.

'You've got a cheek, askin' me that,' Delbert said. 'No complaints so far. Why not travel Economy? Lot less conspicuous than Business and save you a fortune in air fares.'

Leo groaned, seeing all his creature comforts being chiselled away. 'I'll pay you half now and the rest on delivery.' He had an uncomfortable moment as he imagined returning to find no one here — his own passport as well as the money vanished into thin air.

Delbert hesitated, wanting to argue the point but decided against it, taking Rosalie's passport photographs instead. 'Give me two days. Come back on Thursday — same time, same place. Oh, an' give my regards to Harry.'

'Harry? I don't think I'll be seeing him again. Not this time around.'

'Gotcha!' Delbert grinned, pointing snake fingers at him and making Leo realize he'd fallen into one of the oldest traps in the book. 'Always pays to pretend to know more than you do.' He winked. 'See you Thursday, then.'

Leo could scarcely wait for the time to pass but Rosalie behaved like a tourist, enjoying all the delights of Rome. Leo couldn't help but be infected by her enthusiasm.

When they returned to the mean little street behind the delicatessen, Leo was impressed by the excellent job Delbert had made of the forged passport. He also felt a bit guilty. Without a doubt, the man would have seized the opportunity to copy his own passport and, in time, pass that copy on to somebody else. He had crossed so many lines for Rosalie. Prior to meeting her, he had never done anything illegal before in his life.

★ ★ ★

With passports safely in hand, they could at last book into a modest hotel prior to leaving

174

for Australia. Fortunately, Emirates had a cancellation in Business Class so that they could fly out in just three days' time.

Having had little opportunity to watch television before, as her uncle's farm had been too remote for good reception and few of the circus people had time for it, Rosalie was entranced, like a child with a new toy. She watched anything and everything from bullet trains in Japan to wild animals in Africa and welcomed advertisements with equal enthusiasm.

'We should buy those chocolates, Leo! Leo, I really need this special shampoo!'

For the most part he ignored her comments although, turning his mind towards returning home, he knew something would have to be done about Rosalie's clothes. She had come to him with a few things hastily thrown together and underwear that had been washed so many times, it was looking the worse for wear. Not realizing she might be offended, he offered her money to buy some more.

'No, Leo, you do enough for me,' she said, shaking her head and pushing his hand away.

'Rosalie, please take it,' he insisted. 'The clothes you are wearing are almost threadbare. You can't turn up in Melbourne looking like a homeless person. I'll have enough explaining to do as it is.'

'Of course.' Rosalie clapped her hand to her mouth. 'You have wife! She will think bad things of me.'

'No, Rosalie, I don't have a wife. If I did, I'd have told you before.'

'Ohh.' Rosalie paused, digesting this information. 'I see. There were some of the clowns at the circus who loved only men . . .'

'No!' Leo sighed, rolling his eyes. 'I'm so tired of people thinking anyone single at my age is probably gay!'

'I am sorry, Leo. I didn't mean to be rude.'

'No, *I'm* sorry, Rosalie. I shouldn't have bitten your head off like that. I'm not married because I haven't met the right person as yet. And I can promise you one thing — I'll know at once when I do.'

Rosalie didn't think much about this remark at the time but later those words would return to haunt her.

'But I do have a housekeeper,' Leo went on to say. 'A very proper German lady who is a marvellous cook. She came to us when my mother got sick and stayed on to look after me. I know you'll love her because she's kindness itself. Also she has a son, Jake, not much older than you are.'

'Oh, Leo, there's so much of your life I

don't know. You tell me of stables and horses but not of your household — not until now.'

'Like I said, Hannah likes to see things done properly so she'll expect any relative of mind to arrive with luggage, containing underwear and respectable clothes. At least let me give you some money to buy some.' He reached for his wallet again but Rosalie gestured that he should put it away.

'No, Leo. I pay for my clothes with money from Grandfather.' Her smile was sly. 'So you can't tell me what to buy.'

'All right but take something for backup in case you need more. Clothes are expensive in Rome. Buy some underwear, night clothes and something suitable for wearing around the stables. And don't get carried away like most teenagers with spandex and glitter. I don't want to see you looking like a tuppenny whore.'

'What's a — '

'Never mind. I shouldn't have said that. Remember you'll need a jacket as well as good boots, scarves and other warm things. Melbourne can be chilly at this time of year.'

'But it's June.'

'Precisely. We have our winter just now.'

She rolled her eyes. 'Where am I going? Australia is upside-down place in more ways than one.'

She was gone so long that Leo was starting to worry but finally she turned up in a taxi with so many parcels and bags that the driver had to help her to bring them into the hotel. Eyes sparkling with pleasure, she insisted on unpacking and showing him all her purchases, making him realize how quickly she could be turned from a destitute waif into a young woman who loved to shop. Surprisingly, none of her purchases was frivolous; she had spent wisely and well. All she needed now was a large suitcase to accommodate all her new things. She had also taken the time to visit a hairdresser and now sported a modern, spiky haircut that she hoped would give her a sophisticated, modern look. Instead, it made her seem younger than ever. Leo thought it looked awful, too, but was tactful enough not to say so. He comforted himself with the thought that hair always grows.

And, finally, they were almost on their way, waiting in the new Emirates Lounge at Fiumicino for their flight to be called. Rosalie settled back into one of the comfortable seats to read a newspaper someone had left behind while Leo went to get a beer for himself and a soft drink for her.

He returned to find her curled in the chair, hugging her knees and shaking with sobs as tears poured unchecked down her face.

'Rosalie! What's the matter?' he said, jumping immediately to the wrong conclusion. 'Look, if you've changed your mind about leaving Italy, we'll think of something else. You really don't have to . . . '

Vehemently, she shook her head. Giving way to a fresh storm of tears and still unable to speak, she tapped the article in the paper that she had been reading.

Being a modern man who didn't carry a fresh, laundered handkerchief for the comfort of damsels in distress, Leo grabbed a handful of napkins from a dispenser and thrust them into Rosalie's hands. Then he gave his attention to the article she had been reading. It took him a while as he had to translate it while he read but he soon understood it must concern her grandfather's death, describing the unpleasant discoveries that had been made when the authorities uncovered the various crimes at the villa.

The body of local philanthropist, Angelo Barcelona — an assumed name according to some — was recently found in his villa in Sicily. He had been savagely murdered and left in a pool of his own

179

blood. The villa was otherwise deserted and it seems his body lay undiscovered for some days . . .

Leo looked up at Rosalie. Until now he had only half believed some of the wild tales she had told him.

'This was your grandfather?' he said. She nodded, still unable to speak. 'But Rosalie, you already knew this had happened and didn't seem nearly so upset before.' With her face half buried in the napkins, she gestured for him to read on.

Several of the old man's loyal servants were found butchered as well, including Trizia Barcelona, thought by some to be the old man's illegitimate child. Most of the young woman's fingernails were missing and it was obvious that she had been subjected to torture before she died.

'Trizia,' Rosalie managed at last to speak through her shivering and sobs. 'She was my only friend. She gave me scooter. I was so afraid something bad would happen to her. I wanted her to leave with me but she wouldn't because of her boyfriend. Oh, Leo, it's all my fault. Trizia is dead because of me.'

Leo crouched before her, taking her cold,

wet hands in his own. He didn't care that people were staring at them, wondering what was wrong. 'Rosalie, you have no idea what was going on in that house. Did Trizia ever tell you that she was the old man's daughter?'

'No. She let me think she was jus' housemaid.'

'Francesco and his father were taking over your grandfather's business — his throne, for want of a better word. Your friend's death might have nothing to do with you — nothing at all.'

'No.' Rosalie shivered, her expression bleak. 'She died trying to protect me.'

Just at that moment their flight was called and people were suddenly all activity, gathering their belongings and forming a line, ready to board the plane. Rosalie blew her nose fiercely into the last of the napkins, threw them on the table and stood up.

'You're quite sure about this?' Leo said. 'Because it isn't too late to change your mind. You do want to come with me to Australia? Maybe never to return?'

'Yes, Leo.' She managed a watery smile. 'I am sure. If something so evil can happen to Trizia for no reason, I no wish to stay in Italy now. I come to Australia with you.'

9

Australia

Having so much to think about, including the unexpected death of her friend, Rosalie could take no pleasure in the long flight to Australia. At any other time she would have been thrilled by such a journey, especially as they were travelling Business Class. Raised on her uncle's farm in the depths of the countryside, treats had been few and far between — maybe a bar of sweet-smelling soap for her birthday or a cake grudgingly baked by Mancia. Neither her uncle nor his wife believed in pampering anyone; they considered frugal living was good for the soul. Certainly, she'd had a taste of luxury in her grandfather's home but that hadn't ended well, either. Seeing her listless, thoughtful and often close to tears, Leo was quick to divine the cause.

'Rosalie, you can't go on taking the blame for what happened to Trizia; there could be other issues — her death might have nothing to do with you. That house held a lot more secrets than you'll ever know.'

'I suppose so.' Rosalie shrugged, far from comforted and still unable to meet his gaze.

'And you need to look to the future now and think of what to say when we arrive in Oz. It's one thing to get past Italian Customs with a fake passport but the Australian Customs officers know what they're looking for and may not be so easily fooled. If anyone starts asking questions, leave the talking to me. I don't want them to find out your English isn't so good.'

'That's not what you say before. You say my English very good.'

'And so it is for someone taught by a circus performer. But you don't really sound like a girl born in Oz.'

He needn't have worried. The customs officers, flushed with success after a drug bust in the early hours of the morning, stamped their passports and waved them through without so much as a second glance.

Joe Clifton, Leo's stable foreman, was at the airport to meet them, eager to bring the boss up to date with all that had happened while he was away. Although they had been in touch by telephone on a regular basis, there was still a lot to discuss. On the journey home, Leo had talked about Joe in glowing terms but on meeting him Rosalie found him to be a much younger man than she expected, not really good-looking but with an open, friendly face.

He had news of his own, too. In Leo's absence he had married, rather in haste, adding that his new wife was already expecting twins. Somewhat bashful about it, he told Leo this news quickly, not expecting Rosalie to understand. After seating her in the back of the car, Joe largely ignored her, accepting Leo's explanation that she was a member of his extended Italian family; that is until he mentioned that she was to work in the stables. By this time they were on the motorway, travelling back to the city.

'I dunno, boss,' he muttered, turning the rear view mirror to glance at Rosalie. 'Things could be done differently overseas an' I don't have time to train a new kid from scratch. An' I half promised a job to Hannah's son, Jake — he's leaving school jus' now — you know he's been workin' part time in the holidays. Can't see my way clear to take on two newbies.'

'You'll find a way round it, Joe,' Leo said easily, clapping the man on the shoulder. 'You always do.'

Sighing, Joe kept his eyes on the road, shaking his head. Rosalie wanted to say that horses were horses the world over but in view of Joe's stony expression, she thought it best to keep silent. Travelling through a central business district that seemed small after the sprawl of Rome, she would have liked to pause and take in some of the sights of this new and very different world. But Leo wasn't about to indulge her. Now he was almost home, his responsibilities crowded in on him and he wanted to get there as soon as possible. Rosalie would have liked to explore this very different city and ride on one of the old-fashioned trams that rattled around the centre of Melbourne. She wanted to explore the numerous parks and gardens surrounding the city and to see at close quarters these very different plants and trees. Even the air tasted different, scented with eucalypt.

The buildings fascinated her, too. Some were Victorian and others, left over from the early twentieth century, stood alongside the modern 'glass palaces'. What a joy this little city would have been to her erstwhile tutor — all those museums and galleries so close to the city centre. Sadly, she remembered she had lost contact with him entirely. By leaving in such haste, she'd had no time to exchange addresses or even to say goodbye. Only now did she realize how completely she had been cut off from her old life in Italy. She could see there was much to embrace and enjoy in this country but it would take time to make the adjustment.

Leo plunged straight into work as soon as they arrived at the homestead and stables on the outskirts of Melbourne, leaving Rosalie in the care of Hannah, his housekeeper, a smiling, warm-hearted lady who brought domestic order and home-cooking to his bachelor residence. Hannah had questions enough, making Rosalie grateful that Leo had no wife to wonder about the sudden appearance of a relative who had never been mentioned before.

But another surprise awaited her; one that brought her down to earth with a jolt. As Leo's relative, she thought she would be accepted at once, as she had been at her grandfather's villa. Instead, she was disappointed to find herself largely ignored by the other young people who worked in the stables. They assumed her to be a spoilt brat, employed only because she was related to Leo. The only person to make her welcome, having some empathy for her situation, was Leo's housekeeper, Hannah Bauer. Born in Germany and having experienced some prejudice as a migrant herself, she understood Rosalie's problems and took the girl under her wing, making a special pet of her.

Unfortunately, this didn't sit well with Jake, her son, who had been a casual worker in the stables during his school holidays. He felt he had paid his dues and waited long enough to join the permanent staff and resented this new girl who could walk in and become his equal just because she was related to Leo. Nor could he help feeling jealous when Rosalie diverted his mother's attention away from himself. As an only child, he was used to being the centre of Hannah's world and he didn't like to share. He heard them laughing together often, sharing women's secrets that excluded him and he overheard his mother saying one day, 'A son is a fine thing and I love my Jake — well, of course I do. But I know that one day he will marry and leave me. I've always longed for a daughter like you, *liebling*.'

Undeniably handsome, Jake spent a lot of time working out and it showed. He walked like a panther, lithe and muscular, his thick fair hair shone like gold in the sun and he had a pair of astonishing, cornflower-blue eyes and a set of perfect teeth, although his smiles were few. Attracted at first by his Aryan good looks, Rosalie quickly developed a crush but that didn't last for long. Born in Queensland and raised in Melbourne, Jake was all Aussie, having no trace of his mother's accent. He lost no time in mocking Rosalie, teasing her mercilessly for her misuse and bad pronunciation of English words. But he took care to do this only when they were alone; he was all sunshine and smiles when his mother was around.

But no matter how rude he was, Rosalie let his insults wash over her, pretending that she didn't care; if she didn't respond, she hoped he would tire of the game and exercise his malice elsewhere. Jake assumed this was because she didn't understand what he said but after the cruel treatment she had received at the circus, his petty remarks didn't touch her.

Joe Clifton, on the other hand, was agreeably surprised. She certainly knew her way around horses, having an uncanny rapport and almost a sixth sense about what was needed. Tack would be cleaned and polished even before he could draw breath to request it and she got on with the job, never waiting for somebody else to muck out a stable. For sure, some of the old hands resented her, saying she was no more than a new broom, working hard just now to curry favour but Joe saw at once that she had that rare quality, a real affinity with these wayward, often temperamental beasts. He knew Jake resented her but chose not to interfere, thinking it best to let the two of them work out their differences on their own.

The only time he found her close to tears was when she came across the little Shetland pony kept as a companion for a skittish colt by the name of Romeo's Secret. The colt was a newcomer from Tasmania, purchased by owners with more money than sense and delivered to Leo to knock into shape. Joe was already thinking it might be an expensive mistake. Neither his pony companion nor the process of gelding had mellowed the colt's unpredictable nature; he hated everyone and everything, encouraging the little Shetland to behave badly as well; they would both kick or bite without warning or provocation. But, although Rosalie's throat tightened with tears when she first set eyes on that little pony, she found the words to tell Joe that she had once owned such a pony although she couldn't bring herself to mention the circus or how Beppo met his end. This new pony would be recompense enough.

'My heart beat so fast when I see him,' she said, tapping her chest. 'I think Beppo come back to me from the dead. But now I look closer, he isn't the same.'

'Ah well.' Awkwardly Joe patted her on the shoulder, grateful that she hadn't succumbed to her tears. 'They do say that everyone has a double on the other side of the world. Why not animals, too?'

'And this pony — what is his name, Joe?'

'He doesn't have one. We just call him Pest,' Joe said, suppressing a snort of laughter. 'And he's tolerated only because he keeps Romeo calm. You can't trust him — he'll bite you soon as he looks at you if he gets the chance.'

'You should let me try!' Rosalie said, knowing she'd have to do something and soon.

'No way do you go anywhere near those two!' Joe said.

'You can't call that dear little animal Pest — I won't let you,' Rosalie said. 'No wonder he hates everyone.' And before Joe could stop her, she opened the gate and went into Romeo's stall where the big black horse was standing alongside the Shetland pony.

'No!' Joe shouted, making her turn and frown at him, pressing a finger to her lips.

'Oh, you are a beauty, aren't you?' Ignoring Romeo, she spoke to the little horse softly in Italian. 'I shall look after you and comb out the tangles in your mane and tail. Then I'll call you Beppo after my lost friend . . .'

Having heard Joe cry out, several hands had come over to see what was happening. Joe rolled his eyes at them and Jake smirked, waiting for Rosalie to get a taste of the rough treatment usually meted out by the little horse. Instead, everyone was surprised to see the pony pressing against her and nuzzling her pockets, looking for treats. She found a packet of mints and offered one which was accepted eagerly. Then she put her arms around the little horse's neck and embraced him.

'I must go now, I have work to do,' she told him, still in Italian. 'But I'll come back and see you very soon.' She hadn't even looked at Romeo who was ignoring everyone, engrossed in his hay-bag.

She emerged from the stall to murmurs of approval and a round of soft applause. She smiled at everyone, knowing she'd won them over at last. Everyone except Jake who turned away, scowling and disappointed in the way things had turned out. Never mind. Rosalie would keep. He would soon find a way to show her up and everyone would see he was right about her.

The opportunity arose more quickly than he expected. Because Rosalie was the only one to get on with the princely Romeo's Secret as well as his Shetland companion, she was put in sole charge of their feeding and grooming. Romeo's track rider, Nikki Morgan, praised Rosalie's methods, saying the big black horse was a reformed character these days and ready to concentrate on his work. He was starting to do well in his trials and she told Leo he would be ready to go to the track quite soon and even compete in the Spring Carnival if his campaign went as well as she expected.

As more people praised and appreciated Rosalie's efforts, the more Jake's resentment grew and he was determined to bring about her downfall. He saw his opportunity when a new consignment of feed was delivered. Leo and Joe were away at the track and everyone occupied elsewhere, so he and Rosalie were the only ones there to receive it when it arrived. Each animal had his own particular recipe that was to remain unchanged. Leo himself had emphasized this to Rosalie, saying that a digestive upset could be the least of their troubles if there were any sudden changes in the diet of any horse. And because Romeo's Secret was known to be skittish and excitable, his food was monitored closely and his intake of oats reduced.

Aware of Jake's hostility, Rosalie was going about her business and staying out of his way until he surprised her by offering to make coffee for both of them. She smiled and nodded, hoping his attitude towards her could be changing. But less than half an hour after drinking the coffee and before she had finished her careful preparation of the feed for Romeo's Secret, she felt an urgent need to go to the toilet and had to remain there for some time with severe stomach cramps.

'Oh dear,' Jake said, feigning concern when she rejoined him in the store room. 'What happened to you? Was it something you ate?'

'What did you do to me?' Immediately, she was suspicious. 'I never get cramps like that.'

'Spare me the details.' Jake wrinkled his nose. 'If you've got women's problems, I don't need to know.'

He turned his back on her and Rosalie couldn't help feeling that something might be wrong. But what? She took a good look at the feed she had been preparing for Romeo's Secret and although it appeared to be quite OK, she was almost tempted to toss it and start over. But what if nothing was wrong? What would Joe say if she threw good food away for no reason? In the end, she decided her dislike of Jake was making her paranoid so she ignored these disquieting feelings and offered the feed to Romeo's Secret.

The colt was due to race at Flemington the following day. This was to be his first outing on a city track; a high profile jockey had been hired to ride him and both Joe and Leo were excited about his prospects.

Covertly, Jake watched what Rosalie was doing, holding his breath as she hesitated before giving the colt his feed. He knew she was suspicious and hoped she wouldn't notice the extra oats he had crushed to make them look less bulky. He wasn't thinking of the possible harm to the horse, only of the trouble Rosalie would face if Romeo's Secret was found to be unfit to race the next day.

Excited about being taken to town with the team, Rosalie promised herself she would get up earlier than usual for this important occasion. Both Leo and Romeo's owners were anticipating a good result and Rosalie was proud to be travelling with him and to lead him around the mounting yard before the race. She meant to be well rested before getting up in the early hours to travel with her charge.

Scarcely an hour past midnight the household was raised by a hammering at the back door. It was Joe Clifton who had elected to take the place of the night watchman before such an important race; the regular man was elderly and tended to fall asleep. So when Leo went to answer the door, having pulled on a track suit, Joe wasted no time in summoning him to the stables.

'I've already sent for the vet and he's on his way. Romeo's scouring badly and trying to lie down. Someone must have got at him — that's all I can think. And it's serious, Leo.

I think he's very sick.'

Rosalie had also appeared by now, tying a dressing gown around her nightgown and blinking the sleep from her eyes. 'I'll come with you,' she whispered. 'Keep Beppo occupied.'

At the stables, Beppo was standing next to the big horse, guarding him until Rosalie was able to coax him away to an empty stall nearby. All the same, he was stubborn and reluctant to leave. Shortly afterwards, the vet arrived to examine the sick animal, afterwards conferring with Leo and Joe.

'Thank goodness you found him, Joe, and called when you did. If you'd waited much longer it could have been worse. All the same,' he said, shaking his head, 'there'll be no racing for this bloke today.'

'But what happened, Doc?' Leo was thinking of the disappointed owners who would have to be told the horse was scratched. They were difficult people at the best of times and he wasn't looking forward to it.

'Dunno.' The vet shrugged. 'Usually, when these things happen, it's a mix-up with the feed. Who takes care of him?'

'Rosalie, my — er — she's from Italy,' Leo said. 'But she's always so careful and conscientious — I doubt if — '

'I'll take it away and get it analyzed.' The

vet frowned. 'Because we need to get to the bottom of this. Make sure it wasn't sabotage. Prohibited substances are a big issue these days.'

Leo looked stricken. 'Sabotage? But I know all my staff and I trust them — who on earth would want to?'

'I don't know, Leo. But if you have someone here who doesn't wish you well, we need to find out.'

★ ★ ★

'The good news is that there was no prohibited substance.' The vet announced his findings a day or so later to Leo and Rosalie. 'But whatever happened to Romeo was no accident, and you must have been careless preparing his feed.'

'Never,' Rosalie was quick to defend herself. 'I know how important it is. I measured his feed just as I always do.'

'Think, Rosalie. Is it possible you measured the same ingredients twice? It's easily done. Did anything happen to distract you?'

'No, but — ' Rosalie paused, frowning and biting her lip.

'If there's anything we should know, you must tell us right now.' The vet fixed her with a stern look.

She looked from one to the other with a heavy heart. 'I don't know for sure,' she said. 'It's just a suspicion I have.' And she told them about the coffee Jake had offered and the upset stomach that followed, causing her to break off before giving Romeo his feed. 'But I don' think Jake would risk hurting him jus' to make me look bad. The horse could have died.'

All three men tackled Jake and, because it was such a serious accusation, Hannah was invited to be present but warned not to interrupt or to interfere. Jake was truculent at first, folding his arms and rocking on his heels.

'It's that little bitch you brought home from Italy,' he said, lifting his chin at Leo. 'She makes a mistake and half kills your horse but you'd still rather take her word over mine.'

'Never mind that, Jake,' Leo said softly, holding on to his temper. 'Tell us the truth as you see it. We need to get to the bottom of this to make sure it can't happen again.'

'It may well. Because your niece is a ditz who hasn't the first idea what she's doing around a major thoroughbred stable. Where does she come from, anyway? Some dirt farm in the depths of the Italian countryside.' He put on a mock Italian accent. 'How well does she speaka da English? Not very.' He turned on Leo. 'An' you — you're as much to blame for trusting her with too much responsibility.'

'Jake, that's enough.' In spite of being sworn to silence, Hannah felt bound to intervene. 'How can you disrespect Leo like this when he's been so good to us?'

'Good to us?' Jake sneered at his mother. 'Is that what you think? You keep his house like a palace and work like a Victorian servant for the miserable pittance he pays you.'

'Housekeeping is the only skill I have. We are respected here and live in his house like family — '

Jake gave a bark of laughter, shaking his head. 'How deluded can you be?'

'Excuse me but we're rather straying from the point,' the vet cut across this latest argument. 'The purpose of this meeting is to discover exactly what happened to Romeo's Secret. I don't think you realize, Jake, exactly how serious this is. The colt didn't just have a digestive upset. He might have died.'

'Exactly.' Jake unfolded his arms to point at Leo. 'Because you left a valuable animal in the care of that silly girl.'

'I'm sorry, Leo,' Hannah said yet again. 'I know you said I was to sit in on this meeting and not speak but I can't keep silent while my son is behaving without honour to throw suspicion on Rosalie.' So saying, she took a small bottle of pills from her pocket and set it on the desk before them.

'These were prescribed for me a while ago. I took some as I needed them and should have discarded the rest but I didn't. And when Rosalie complained of a stomach upset at such a crucial time, it set me thinking. Had my pills remained where I left them, I'd have thought no more of it.' She paused, looking round at her audience to make sure she had their attention. 'But instead I found the bottle in my son's room and half the pills missing.'

'Of course you did, Ma.' Jake raised his eyes heavenwards. 'I don't tell you every time I suffer from constipation.'

'Now everything begins to make sense.' The vet pounced on his words. 'The analysis of the horse's feed showed an excessive portion of oats — and a minute quantity of a human aperient, available only on prescription. How could you imagine we wouldn't find out?'

'Oh, Jake.' Hannah closed her eyes. 'To think you would ruin your life in this way — and mine.'

'This is so unfair!' Unwilling to believe the evidence against him was overwhelming, Jake continued to bluster. 'I've been set up here!'

'No, Jake,' Leo said softly. 'The only person working a set-up is you. You were trying to incriminate Rosalie.' He sat back to look at the lad. 'Doesn't it even matter to you that the horse might have died?'

'Well, he didn't, did he?' Jake said, leaving the room without permission and slamming the door behind him. Moments later, they heard him start up the motorbike his mother had bought for his recent eighteenth birthday and ride furiously away from the stables.

In the midst of the shocked silence that followed, Hannah burst into tears.

★ ★ ★

Jake didn't leave without any purpose in mind; he knew exactly where he was going. Bored by most girls his own age who chattered about boy bands all the time, he found older women much more of a challenge. His latest conquest was a divorced woman well over thirty and ripe for a fling with a younger man. And although he didn't tell a direct lie, he let her think he was at least twenty. Tall and muscular as he was, it wasn't that hard to believe. She called herself Adele — although he suspected that wasn't her real name — and lived in a smart studio apartment on St Kilda Road near the city. He knew she worked as a wardrobe mistress for one of the theatre companies but didn't care enough to ask which one. They met through a girl he had been dating before and things had grown hot and heavy between them that very first night. Tiny and fragile-looking, Adele surprised him by being a tigress in the sack; he had to throw away the shirt he had worn that night as it was covered in bloodstains from the scratches her dark, red nails had left on his back.

Although Hannah knew that her son was like catnip to some girls, she had no idea how he spent those evenings in town, believing he went to movies or clubs and stayed over with an old school friend. So she teased him, assuming he had many girls and telling herself there must be safety in numbers. If she were to suspect the truth, Jake knew she wouldn't approve.

He thought about all this as he rode towards town. After siding with Leo, Hannah deserved to worry and wonder where he had gone. He had been just a small boy when she took the post as Leo's housekeeper. In those days he had entertained a fantasy that Leo would fall in love with Hannah and ask her to marry him so that he, Jake, would become their son and heir. It never occurred to him that, aside from being much older than Leo,

Hannah was neither glamorous nor sophisticated enough to appeal to him. And now, although that fantasy had long evaporated, he had been annoyed when the boss returned from Italy with Rosalie in tow — a new cuckoo in the nest.

Festering on all this, he ate a hamburger and chips at a McDonald's and waited until it was late enough to be sure that Adele would be home. She answered the intercom yawning and sounding tired, although she perked up immediately when she knew it was Jake.

'Jake — hello! What a nice surprise.' She pressed the button to let him come up and ran to put on her sexy dressing gown, discarding the comfortable one she had been wearing before. No time for make-up, so she smiled at herself in the mirror, pinching her cheeks to give them some colour and prinking her hair. This evening was going to be fun, after all.

★　★　★

'What's happened?' she said much later as they lay in bed, sated. 'You seem a bit tense tonight.'

'You know me so well,' he said, snuggling into the soft, downy pillows of her king-sized bed. 'If it's OK with you, Adele, I'll be here for some time. I've left home.'

'Ohh,' Adele breathed out the word, looking thoughtful.

★ ★ ★

Jake's disappearance caused both Leo and his mother some concern. Rosalie couldn't help feeling partly responsible for his departure. It was Hannah's affection for her that had triggered his jealousy, making him take such drastic action against her. Inevitably, a certain reserve had sprung up between the two women, clouding the happy relationship they had shared before.

When Jake still hadn't returned home after three days, Leo waited until Rosalie had gone to the stables before raising the subject of her missing son.

'I'm so sorry, Hannah, but he took off without giving us the chance to talk it through.'

'I don't understand him sometimes. So ungrateful to you, so possessive of me.' Hannah put a handkerchief to her damp eyes. 'It's no excuse but before we came here, we had no one to love or depend upon but each other. I made a mother's boy of him, I suppose.'

'I wasn't going to sack him,' Leo said. 'He

must have learned his lesson after the fright we all had. I'd have given him a flea in the ear and let him stay.'

'Oh, Leo, you are too good,' Hannah wept again. 'So understanding of stupid youths.'

'Well, I'm concerned for the lad and I hope he's with friends — good friends. I shouldn't like him to fall into bad company.'

Hannah sighed. 'I'm afraid he might be the bad company other young men will fall into,' she said. 'He has always been headstrong and rather uncaring — perhaps he takes after his father.'

Leo sat back, realizing how much he had taken Hannah for granted and how little he knew about this woman who had become such an integral part of his life. 'You've never told me about your husband, Hannah.'

'That's easy. Because there wasn't one. Not here in Australia, anyway. My parents were business people in Germany and it suited them to marry me to a colleague of theirs when I was very young. I didn't mind. I thought it glamorous to be married when most of my friends were still at school or college. But he was a cruel man, much older than I, and it pleased him to beat me regularly when he was drunk.'

'Oh, Hannah.'

'When I told my father what was

happening, he said it was normal, that a lot of men beat their wives and I'd better get used to it. I wanted to leave but I was too scared — not even my mother was brave enough to help me. One night, when it was raining and my husband was out late as usual, he drove his car off the docks and into the sea. I felt nothing but relief when they told me. I was free of that tyrant at last.'

Leo sat back, fascinated, waiting for her to continue this tale that he hadn't heard before. 'And that's when you came here to Australia? Surely, as your husband's widow, you must have inherited — '

'Next to nothing at all. His money was all tied up in his business and his partners made sure they held on to it. But I was determined to get away; I was no longer naïve and wouldn't allow myself to be married to suit my parents again. I had no money of my own so I had to steal from my father to buy a cheap flight to Australia. Migrants from Europe were welcome in those days. Even penniless ones.' She shrugged and smiled. 'The rest you know.'

'Not quite everything. What about Jake?'

Hannah's expression softened. 'Yes, Jake. The child of my middle years. Just as I thought I was too old for motherhood.' She smiled, shaking her head. 'I was working as a cook-housekeeper on a cattle station in Queensland. Jake's father was a guest in the house where I worked — he should have been a comedian the way he made everyone laugh. People warned me, saying that he was no good but that just made him seem more interesting. I always knew he'd never be mine.'

'Because he was married already?'

'Very much so and with kids. You know what people say? Past a certain age, all the good ones are married or gay.' She smiled, remembering. 'My heart just stopped when I saw him — it was love at first sight. Thick hair that shone like gold, the bluest of eyes and, best of all, he was from Hamburg, too. It was lovely to speak my native language again and remember places we both knew. He was thinking of buying a property that was for sale nearby but that didn't come to anything. I like to think that he really loved me, too, because when we parted he was crying as hard as I was. But I always knew I'd never see him again. I didn't know I was expecting Jake until he was long gone.'

'But surely if he loved you, he'd want to know about the child. Your employers must have known how to get in touch with him.'

'What for? I had no intention of spoiling the life he had. Our love was a brief moment of madness — and we knew it — but my reward was Jake.'

'Who is bringing grief home to you now.'

'Oh, well,' she smiled ruefully. 'Maybe my lack of virtue is having its own reward.'

'Do you want me to try and find him? Make sure he's OK?'

'No, Leo.' She sighed. 'Let him be. He took off in a temper with no clothes and no money. He'll have to come back before long.'

⋆ ⋆ ⋆

She was right. A chastened Jake was already on his way home. Adele had thrown him out and he was recalling their last bitter exchange. Familiarity had indeed bred contempt. Tired, after a full working day and evening at the theatre, Adele had returned home to find him lying on the couch with the television blaring and her normally pristine apartment a total shambles.

'Time we had a talk.' She switched off the television and stood in front of it, hands on hips.

'Why did you do that, Del? I was watching the show.'

'Too bad. I need your full attention. You've eaten everything in the fridge with no thought of replacing it and this place is a mess. What are you going to do, Jake? When are you going to put your life back in order?'

'I don't know. I thought you'd look after me — '

'Me? I'm not your mother, Jake. You didn't even bring a change of clothes. You've been wearing the same things for three days now and they're starting to smell.'

'I wash every day.'

'Oh, I know. Leaving wet towels all over the bathroom floor. I want my life back and I need you out of here now. Not in the morning. Tonight.'

'Fair go — it's nearly midnight. An' I don't have enough money to put any gas in the bike.'

Frowning, Adele scrabbled in her purse, produced a fifty dollar note and threw it at him. 'Heaven save me from sponging schoolboys,' she muttered.

'I'm not a schoolboy.'

'Not far from it. Monica told me you're only eighteen. Why didn't you say so before?'

'It didn't come up. You were too busy ripping my pants off to ask.'

'Out!' she yelled. 'Get out right now. An' don't bother to call me again.'

★ ★ ★

Hannah didn't hear him come home and didn't know he was back until she spotted his motorbike outside first thing in the morning. Then she heard him opening drawers and banging about in his room. When she went upstairs to see what was happening, she found him stuffing clothes into the good travelling bag Leo had given her for Christmas. He didn't look up when she stood in the doorway, watching him.

'Where are you going, Jacob?' she said softly.

'None of your business,' he muttered, scowling. 'And stop calling me Jacob — you know I don't like it.'

'Well, you're eighteen now, so you can do as you please.' She sighed. 'I have fifty dollars in my purse. You can have that to help you on your way — '

'Fifty dollars?' he sneered. 'I'd get a long way on that, wouldn't I?'

'Jake, don't do anything hasty. We can get past this if we can only sit down and discuss it. Leo's not angry — not any more.'

'So Leo's not angry. That makes everything perfect, doesn't it?'

'Jake, you don't seem to understand. You are the one in the wrong here.'

'Right! Wrong! I'm bored with all these rules and regulations.' Jake forced the bag shut, zipped it and turned to leave although his mother still stood in the doorway, barring his path.

'Goodbye, Ma.' He picked her up and lifted her easily out of his way. 'I don't think we'll be seeing each other any time soon.'

'But Jake, how will you manage? Where are you going? How will you live?'

Instead of answering, he turned to give her a cheery salute and ran downstairs as she sat slumped on his bed. Moments later, she heard the motorbike roar into action before speeding away. She had the feeling she might never see him again. But instead of feeling sad and bereft as she expected, she was surprised to feel a curious sense of relief.

It was some time before she went to put money into her savings account. Only then did she discover that her son had stolen her bank card and used it to remove all her savings over several weeks. But instead of reporting the theft, she kept this knowledge to herself. Her son would have a lot of explaining to do if he ever came back.

10

Australia — Three years later

When Rosalie entered the church she saw it was almost filled to capacity, redolent with the scent of women's perfume and wedding flowers. Of course, this was an important society wedding and, although the church was nearly large enough to be called a cathedral, there was scarcely any space left for the riders and other staff from Leo Marino's stables. Leo was a popular boss and the team had turned out in force to see him getting married to Mary Browne. Along with the other late arrivals, Rosalie and his resident track rider, Nikki Morgan, found themselves crammed into one of the last remaining pews at the back of the church. Really, this was the last place she wanted to be but there was no way of avoiding it although she had done her best, saying someone needed to stay behind to look after the horses. But Leo himself had sought her out, insisting that she must be there, not just at the church but at the reception afterwards. Her absence would make her conspicuous and was bound to cause comment, especially as everyone believed them to be related. This was the story they gave out when Leo returned, bringing her with him from Italy, and there had been no reason to change it or let anyone know it was a lie.

'We've been through so much together, Rosalie,' he said, pushing a stray lock of hair away from her face and making her shiver. She could only hope he had no idea how his touch affected her. 'And you're such an asset to the stables, especially in the way you're handling Romeo's Secret. You've made a huge contribution to his success.'

'And happy to do it — always.' She managed a smile. 'But do I really have to come to the wedding, Leo? Crowds make me nervous, even when we go to the races.' She made one last desperate effort to get off the hook. 'And you'll have so many other people wanting to speak to you as well as all of Mary's relatives. It will be such a grand affair — nobody's going to notice if I'm not there.'

'*I'll* notice,' he said, 'and so will Mary. She's very fond of you, you know.'

'Is she?' Rosalie muttered listlessly. 'Well, if you insist, I suppose I must come.'

'Oh, you — you're not as shy as you think.' So saying, he pressed a small envelope into her hand. 'And treat yourself to a nice new dress, as well. I want you to look your best — you're supposed to be my only relative, remember?'

'Oh, Leo.' She sighed, knowing there was no way out of it now and that she sounded less than gracious. 'Thanks.'

But she had learned to be good at hiding her emotions and so far Joe Clifton was the only person to determine the extent of her true feelings for Leo, reading her a stern lecture on the perils of falling in love with someone too closely related. He raised the subject when they were together in Romeo's stall, grooming him before taking him to the track. October was here and the horse had already missed out on a run in the Caulfield Cup which had been won by one of the English raiders but he was now favoured to win the Cox Plate. Leo would have preferred to concentrate on the Spring Carnival, postponing the wedding until early December but Mary's father had already had a small stroke so she wanted the wedding to take place at once while the old man was still well enough to give her away.

Joe wasn't sure how Rosalie was going to react to what he felt bound to say; her temper could be quite frightening if she were sufficiently roused.

'Look, Rosie, I know it's none of my

business but you can't seem to keep your eyes off Leo — especially when you think no one's looking.'

'You're right, Joe. It is none of your business,' she said through gritted teeth and making the horse stamp his foot as she groomed him too hard.

'I'm telling you this for your own good.' Joe wasn't about to let it pass. He was a plain man, used to plain speaking. 'You can't let yourself fall in love with Leo because it's — well, it's not healthy. You need to get out more. Spend some time with people your own age.'

'Thank you, Joe. I know you mean well but I'm all right as I am. You don't understand.'

'I do. I understand only too well. My sister fell in love with one of our cousins and nearly killed herself with an overdose of sleeping pills the night before he got married.'

'Well, I'm not so stupid. I've accepted that Leo's marrying Mary and I'm fine with it. I think they're very well suited,' she said, smiling brightly in the hope of concealing the lie. In fact, she had scarcely recognized her feelings for Leo until Joe had done her the disservice of pointing them out, so the pain in her heart was still fresh — and new.

Studying Leo's back now as he stood before the altar, she could tell he was nervous. He was wearing a dark blue suit that she hadn't seen before. Mary had probably helped him to choose it because it made him look sleek and expensive, quite unlike his casual, rather untidy self. He was standing ramrod straight beside his best man. She didn't recognize that one either so he was probably some relative of Mary's, pressed into service for the day. She knew Leo had no close relatives of his own; not in Australia anyway. From the soft murmur of voices behind him, he must know that the church was filled to capacity with their many friends and business acquaintances as well as the relatives of his bride. He didn't turn round to look.

As they waited what seemed an age for the bride to arrive, Rosalie thought back over the three years that she had been here in Australia and how generously Leo had welcomed her into his home, treating her as if she really were a niece or a cousin, giving her work in his stables and trusting her with his best horses. She had been happy there, particularly since Jake went away.

Considering Leo to be a confirmed bachelor, no one thought he would ever marry and that romance had passed him by. Having a generous nature combined with an unconscious sex appeal, women found him easy to like and perhaps even love but nothing ever came of it. From time to time he might have a girlfriend but if she tried to advance the relationship, Leo would let her down lightly and back away. And now, advancing into his forties and wholeheartedly devoted to his work with the horses, he didn't seem to have room in his life for anything or anyone else.

Until Mary Browne came along and changed everything. Rosalie remembered it well as she had been present on the afternoon that they met.

★ ★ ★

Mary's father — something big in the oil industry — had sent Leo a filly to train. A birthday present for his daughter, he said. But, although there was good breeding behind her, the filly proved to be skittish and almost unbroken so Leo turned her over to Rosalie and Nikki to pull into shape. The filly had been with them for more than a month before Mary drove from the city to see what progress was being made.

When she saw Mary Browne for the first time, Rosalie realized she had never set eyes on a woman of such unusual beauty. A perfect figure encased in a pale blue dress that cost more than most people earned in a week, a perfectly matched string of pearls and an expensive designer handbag on her shoulder. If she wore cosmetics at all, they must have been expensive and subtle as her skin seemed luminous, radiating only natural good health. And, while she was not in the first bloom of youth, her prematurely grey hair was like a white nimbus around her unlined, youthful face. Her eyes were a dark, almost navy blue, full of wonder and good humour at the world around her. Rosalie felt like a grubby urchin in comparison. Other than on a movie screen, she had never seen a woman of such peerless beauty from the top of her well-groomed head to her unsuitable, high-heeled shoes. She must have all the time in the world to spend, to come out looking like that, Rosalie thought, unable to resist a moment of cattiness. Mary Browne surely lived on a different plane. She didn't tumble out of bed in the early hours of the morning to look after horses.

With her gaze fixed only on Leo, Mary had walked the length of the stables towards him, smiling and holding out both her hands in greeting.

'Mr Marino,' was all she had to say in that low, husky voice to make him her devoted slave.

'Miss Browne, I believe.' Leo could scarcely find voice enough to answer her, seeming almost dazed as he received her hands into his own. 'Welcome to the Marino stables.'

The filly, standing beside him, was quite forgotten and Rosalie knew, with certainty and a cold feeling as if a lump of ice had frozen her heart, that Leo was falling in love.

Worse, and what made her more miserable still, she couldn't help liking the woman. How much easier it would have been if Mary had been a bitch and she could detest her. But she was just as sweet and generous as she looked and with always a kind word for Rosalie, including her in their discussions about her horse. At thirty-five and never having been married either, she was exactly the right age for Leo — it would be a marriage made in heaven — or so everyone said.

When her tutor in Italy had given her Hans Christian Andersen's *Fairy Tales* to help with her reading, her favourite story had been *The Little Mermaid;* a tale of self-sacrifice and unrequited love. She had cried over it often and now she could understand why. Today it seemed to mirror her own journey through life. Leo had appeared like a prince, rescuing her when she needed it, bringing her to Australia and allowing her to stay in his home, keeping her close as a pet. But of course he had never thought of her as anything more.

★ ★ ★

The organ struck up with the familiar strains of 'Here Comes the Bride', bringing everyone, smiling, to their feet. The sooner the serious part of the ceremony was over, the sooner champagne could start flowing and the real festivities begin.

For an important wedding such as this, the television people were there in force as well as those employed to record it all for posterity. The bride arrived on her father's arm, standing tall and looking every inch the Toorak princess, her many attendants fussing around her, arranging the veil and the magnificent embroidered lace train attached to her shoulders. With tears of happiness shining in her eyes, Mary looked beautiful as an angel. She even smelled delicious as she passed. Of course she did.

As the wedding service proceeded without a hitch, the rings at last blessed and exchanged, Rosalie reached the decision she had been coming to ever since Mary came into Leo's life and Joe made her face up to her feelings. She could no longer go on like the little mermaid, smiling and hiding her tears. She couldn't remain at the stables, working for Leo, watching his new life unfolding with Mary. Their happiness would be like a knife in her heart every day. The time had come for her to break away from Leo entirely. She would have to move on.

From somewhere a long way off, she could hear the minister saying the familiar, time-honoured phrase, 'You may kiss the bride.'

And Leo did kiss her and with such enthusiasm that it hardened Rosalie's resolution to leave. She couldn't stand by watching them as they fell more and more in love and Mary wasn't too old to have a baby — she might even have two.

Oh, it would be so hard to tear herself away from Romeo's Secret and Beppo, to say nothing of Hannah who would probably feel her loss more than anyone. Jake continued to stay away and nobody knew if he had contacted his mother or even bothered to let her know where he was. Hannah found it hard to speak of him and he had simply disappeared from their lives as if he had never existed.

The bride and groom had walked back down the aisle and were leaving the church now in a hail of confetti. Having arrived late and been placed at the back of the church, Rosalie was one of the first to follow, wondering if anyone would miss her if she were to slip away now and go home.

Mary and Leo posed on the steps of the church while a barrage of photographers jostled for the best position from which to film and photograph the radiant bride and groom, who had eyes for no one but each other. Cars passed in the street below, some almost stopping to smile and wave at the happy couple.

Behind them came a well-polished black car with dark tinted windows concealing whoever might be inside. Seeing it gave Rosalie a cold feeling at once, reminding her of the vehicles which had come to her grandfather's villa bringing those men who had been responsible for his death. Maybe she was the only person to see it for what it was because everyone else was watching the bride and groom. A back window slid down halfway, just far enough for the muzzle of a gun to poke out. To Rosalie, it seemed almost to be happening in slow motion as, before she could shout a warning, three shots rang out in quick succession, making everyone cower and scream before peering around in fright to see who had been hit.

But only one person appeared to have been

the target of the attack and it was Mary, the bride, who collapsed, fatally wounded into her husband's arms, dead even before she hit the ground. She had taken one shot to the head and two others were blooming like red flowers on her chest, a shocking crimson against the pristine white of her gown.

The wedding party witnessed this in stunned amazement, scarcely able to believe that the woman who had been a happy bride just a few moments ago, now lay dead in her husband's arms.

Breaking the horrified silence that followed, Leo's howl of grief seemed scarcely human but it served to galvanize everyone into action. Several people found mobile phones and were trying to summon an ambulance, hoping it might not be too late although everyone standing close by could see that it was.

Rosalie thought of the reception that would never take place now — all those beautiful flowers, the enormous three-tiered wedding cake. Mary's father stumbled forward, falling to his knees beside his daughter who was still lying cradled in Leo's arms. White-faced and trembling, the old man looked as if he were about to have a heart attack or a stroke.

'Why?' he murmured at last. 'Dear God, why would anyone want to hurt Mary? My innocent girl who never wished harm to anyone . . . ' He bit his lips, suppressing his tears, refusing to break down in front of such a crowd. 'I'm just thankful her mother isn't alive to see such a day.'

Hoping to sell their footage to the media, a few callous people continued to film the tragedy until grim-faced ushers rallied and took charge, threatening to confiscate their equipment or break it if they didn't cease. They scattered quickly, unwilling to lose what they had.

When the ambulance arrived, the paramedics gently covered Mary and lifted her inside, confirming that there was nothing more to be done. Her father wanted to go with her and they assisted him aboard while a stunned Leo remained seated at the kerb, his arms resting on his knees and his feet in the gutter, watching the ambulance move slowly away; no need for sirens or urgency now. He looked a mess, his suit and his white shirt covered in Mary's blood. There was even a smear of blood on his face. Joe Clifton, Nikki and Rosalie hovered behind him, feeling helpless and not knowing what to do. It was just as well perhaps that Leo didn't have his own car; a silver service taxi had been booked to take them straight to the airport from the reception. He was the only person to know their honeymoon destination as it was to have been a surprise for Mary.

'This is all my fault,' he whispered. 'I should have remembered — I ought to have known.'

'How could you know, boss?' Joe put a comforting hand on his shoulder. 'That some madman would target your wedding party — '

'This was no madman,' Leo said softly. 'That was an execution. Three shots to make sure. All perfectly planned.'

'You're making no sense, Leo,' Joe said. 'I don't understand.'

Leo took a shuddering breath. 'Too much publicity. I shouldn't have let Mary organize such a high profile society wedding. All those magazine editors chasing her, offering ridiculous sums of money. If only we had eloped or settled for a low-key affair with just family, she might still be alive.'

'But Leo, Mary was thrilled to be marrying you,' Nikki said. 'She told me she was looking forward to everyone being there — her dearest wish was that it should be remembered as the biggest and happiest party of the year.'

'Everyone will remember all right.' He couldn't keep the tears and bitterness from his voice. 'But not for the reasons she wanted.'

Even as his friends sympathized with his plight, he knew it was impossible for them to understand the dark place in which he found himself now. That visit to Sicily had long since faded from his memory but he should have remembered his uncle's thinly veiled threats. He had been told to watch his back and he hadn't. So he was certain this was why Mary had been targeted rather than himself. His uncle had watched and waited until he knew just how to make Leo suffer the most — by slaughtering his bride in front of him on his wedding day.

★ ★ ★

Mary's funeral was just as miserable an event as everyone expected it to be. Her father was in hospital, having succumbed to a further stroke and wasn't expected to live, so there was little point in delaying the funeral for him to be there. Most of the family and friends who had attended the wedding were absent this time, afraid of being caught in the midst of another drive-by shooting.

The police conducted an investigation but with so many unreliable witnesses giving different accounts, there was nothing solid to go on; they had to conclude that it was an unfortunate random attack and no arrests had been made. Leo didn't tell them of his suspicions. The people who committed the crime would have disposed of the weapon at once and were probably at the airport even before the police arrived on the scene. The truth was that he didn't care; he was far too exhausted to think of retaliation or revenge. There would be no miracle. Mary would not be restored to him and only grey, empty days lay ahead.

The funeral took place in the graveyard where an open grave lay waiting for Mary alongside that of her mother. It hadn't rained for days but that day it was pouring, punctuated with thunder, lightning and winds high enough to bring down some trees in the nearby hills. If nothing else, the weather suited Leo's mood. The service was minimal; just a few words conducted by an Anglican minister, anxious to get out of the rain, followed by a tearful, faltering eulogy from Mary's cousin who had been her chief bridesmaid. She kept glancing at Leo, making it all too clear that somehow she thought him to blame for Mary's death. When she finished her speech, she glanced at him, expecting him to say a few words himself but Leo found it beyond him, closing his eyes and shaking his head. He couldn't even bear to throw a flower on to her coffin when it was lowered into the grave.

Rosalie and Joe Clifton were the only ones from the stables to attend, standing on either side of Leo to give their support. The ill feeling emanating from Mary's family group was almost palpable and Rosalie glared back at them, a lioness preparing to defend her own.

Fortunately, rather than attend a funeral feast that would have been awkward, everyone chose to go their separate ways, although Mary's cousin accosted Leo before he left, insisting on having a last word.

'I've been watching you, Leo, and I think you know a lot more about this than you're saying.' She came to stand in his personal space, crowding him. 'You look like a man racked with guilt to me. You know who's responsible for this, don't you? They were *your* enemies, weren't they? It's you — not poor Mary — who should have been murdered in cold blood.'

'Don't you think that's what I wish every wretched night of my life?' Leo's voice cracked with emotion. 'Knowing that I have to face the future without her.'

'You leave him alone.' Rosalie stood between them, fiercely shoving the woman aside. Used to handling wayward horses, her touch wasn't gentle and the woman almost fell. 'Hasn't Leo suffered enough without you heaping coals of fire on his head?'

'My cousin was a saint — '

'Yes, well — saints get martyred, don't they?' Rosalie snapped back.

'Look at him. I don't know what Uncle Will was thinking, pushing her towards a man like Leo Marino. The son of an Italian immigrant involved in horse racing and gambling — probably consorting with criminals. No way was he ever good enough for a beautiful soul like Mary.'

Rosalie felt her temper rising and she took a deep breath, longing to slap the self-satisfied look off the woman's face.

'Rosalie, that'll do,' Leo said softly. 'We're all grieving here and it makes us say things we don't mean. Let it go.'

'But Leo — '

'We're leaving now — let it go.' And glancing at Joe who took Rosalie's other arm, together they almost frog-marched her towards the car.

'If you weren't both so upset that would have been funny,' Joe said, trying to lighten the mood. Leo responded with a wan smile.

Leo's friends and colleagues hoped the funeral would have given him closure and that life might get back to normal but it didn't. He showed little interest in Joe's plans for Romeo's Secret and hadn't been near the stable in days, forcing Joe to come up to the house to tackle him.

'Just do as you like, Joe,' he said, closing his eyes and wincing as if with a headache. 'I'm sure you know best.'

'He missed the Cox Plate but he's still qualified for the Melbourne Cup. But we'll need to stump up the fees if you want him to run — or else it'll be too late.'

Leo sighed and went to the safe in the living room. He took out a bundle of money and tossed it to Joe.

'That was supposed to be cash for the honeymoon. Do as you like with it. I don't care.'

'An' you can't expect Rosalie an' me to cover for you forever. We can do so much but the owners think I'm a bogan and that she's just a kid. It's you they expect to be taking charge of their interests.'

'How many more times, Joe? I DON'T CARE!'

★ ★ ★

They did enter Romeo's Secret in the Melbourne Cup but he went in as a long shot and didn't even place. The Spring Carnival had passed without any significant wins for the stables and Leo remained closeted in his study, poring over the pictures he had on his iPad of Mary and listening to the piano concertos she loved.

Christmas was coming — a season that Hannah had always held dear — so she screwed up her courage and huffed up the several flights of stairs to speak to Leo. Fearing the worst, Rosalie followed, listening outside the door and sure enough it wasn't long before she heard Leo's voice raised in anger.

'You stupid woman! Of course I don't want to celebrate Christmas! I may never celebrate anything ever again!'

With her shoulders shaking, Hannah came out of the room and fell weeping into the younger woman's arms.

'Oh, Rosalie, I don't know what to do for him — not anymore.'

'He doesn't deserve you.'

Rosalie glowered at Leo's study door which remained stubbornly closed. She led Hannah back to the kitchen and made her a cup of strong, sweet tea, seating her in a comfortable chair to drink it. Shocked that Leo should yell at her, which had never happened before, Hannah was still shuddering with the occasional sob. Rosalie looked at her old friend and saw that her clothes didn't fit her these days. No longer plump and happy, Hannah had lost a lot of weight since her son went away and Mary died. Seeing her like this only served to strengthen Rosalie's resolve.

'I've had enough of this, Hannah,' she said. 'We all have our sorrows — you most of all — and I won't let him treat you this way. We've done our best to support him through this tragedy and it was never enough. But he should set it aside now and return to the land of the living.'

'He needs more time, Rosalie. He's still in a very bad place.'

'And things will only get worse if we go on indulging his moods. There's only so much Joe and I can do without him and the business is already on its knees. Even Nikki's threatening to leave. Time he had a wake-up call.' So saying, she ran swiftly upstairs before Hannah could raise any further objections. She threw open the door of Leo's study to find him sitting in semi-darkness, looking thin and hollow-eyed; he hadn't been eating properly for some time.

Rosalie threw back the curtains and opened the windows wide to let in sunshine and fresh air. Dust motes filled the air; Hannah had not been allowed in to clean

Leo's study for weeks. She grabbed the iPad lying in front of him and tossed it into a drawer. Then she switched off his computer, cutting off that mournful piano recital that he kept playing over and over.

'If you can't do it yourself, Leo,' she said, 'I'm declaring this time of mourning officially over.'

'How dare you come up here without being invited — '

'Oh, I dare — when you upset Hannah who has been more than a mother to you. All she wants is to make a nice Christmas for us.'

'I don't want to celebrate anything. Why can't anyone see that I need to be left alone with my grief?'

'Because it's gone on for weeks now and you're bringing everyone else down with you. We've lost two owners already since Mary died and we're about to lose another. If the business fails, it isn't just you, you know. Think of all the people depending on you.'

'So what? There are plenty of other stables — other jobs.' Leo started to shrug.

'Don't you shrug your shoulders at me, Leo Marino. I thought you were a man of courage. A man who could face up to the hard knocks of life — who could rise like a phoenix from the ashes. But instead you cower up here in your room, bleating about your loss. Would Mary be proud of you now? I don't think so.'

He slapped her then. Not hard, just enough to put a stop to those dreadful words that he didn't want to hear.

Rosalie stared at him for a moment, wide-eyed, pressing a hand to her stinging cheek before running from the room.

'Rosalie — wait!' he called after her. 'I'm so sorry. I didn't mean — '

But she didn't stop to hear any more. Half-blinded by tears, she ran to her room, snatched her travelling bag from the wardrobe and started to fill it with clothes — any clothes. Hannah, who had probably overheard most of her exchange with Leo, stood in the doorway, watching her.

'Rosalie, *liebling*,' she said. 'What are you doing? Where will you go?'

'I don't know, Hannah,' she said brokenly. 'I wanted to shake him out of this terrible mourning and I said too much, so he hit me.'

'I heard. But this isn't like Leo.'

'He isn't himself these days and neither am I. But I can't stay here watching him tear down everything we've all built together. He thinks of no one and nothing else but his misery and I hate him!'

'Do you, Rosalie? Really?' Hannah said softly.

'No — I love him — of course I do. But oh, how I wish I didn't. I made up my mind to leave when I saw him getting married to Mary. Then I stayed on because I thought he needed me.'

'But he does, Rosalie. He does.'

She shook her head, giving a tight smile. 'No. But I do understand him, Hannah. He may not know it yet but he's a romantic at heart. It might take a while but he'll find another Mary.' She took a deep breath. 'Fortunately, I still have my passport. I could go anywhere. New Zealand, maybe. Not such hot summers as here. I know about breeding horses and I can make myself useful there.'

'Good. I was afraid you'd go back to Italy.'

'Oh, no.' Rosalie shivered, remembering Francesco and his plans for her. 'I could never go back there.'

'New Zealand is better — not quite so far.'

'Hannah — I hate to ask — but could you lend me some money? Just till I find a job and get settled over there.'

Hannah looked discomfited. 'Oh Rosalie, if I had any money, of course I would. But I'm afraid Jake — Jake took all my savings when he left.'

'Everything? You never told us. How could he do that to you?'

'For him it was easy.' She shrugged. 'I don't

care. The money was for him, anyway — for when he should want to get married or buy a house. He collected it sooner rather than later, that's all.'

'But to take all your money and without asking — leaving you nothing for a rainy day?'

'Well, the sun is shining now, isn't it?' Hannah smiled.

11

Leo apologized gracefully so that Rosalie calmed down and didn't feel the need to escape just yet. Leaving the Marino stables would have meant taking a huge leap into the unknown. All the same, her wake-up call had been enough to shock Leo out of his downward spiral of gloom. He roused himself as if from a long sleep, renewed his interest in the stables, admitting at last that life should go on and he must take charge of his business again. With Leo once more at the helm, Nikki Morgan reversed her decision to leave and some of their established owners renewed the faith by bringing in some new horses. Whenever Leo was feeling sombre, everyone gave him some space and there was life and laughter again around the Marino stables.

Christmas was celebrated with some merrymaking, if not on the lavish scale that Hannah would have liked and in the New Year, Joe gave some thought to the problem of Rosalie and her lack of friends. Married and with a young family, he wanted everyone happy and contented as he was himself and he found a solution with the unwilling assistance of Jenna, his wife, who tried to warn him against interfering in other people's lives. Several of her young cousins had recently come down from Queensland to live nearby and work in the orchards; Joe saw this as the perfect opportunity for the young people to get acquainted.

'You can't force these things, Joe,' Jenna said. 'Just because they're the same age, you think my cousins are suitable but they're just backwoods boys who have no real manners.'

'Rosalie grew up on a farm, too. They'll find something in common.'

'Maybe but girls are usually more mature. My cousins never got much of an education as they moved around all the time. My sister and her husband were new-agers, itinerant fruit pickers, smoking weed and half out of their minds most of the time, letting the boys run wild. They'll have nothing in common with Rosie — she won't even give them a second glance.'

'OK. I get what you're saying but I'll take them all out somewhere — my treat. Then it won't look like a proper date.'

'Well, don't be surprised if it backfires on you,' Jenna said. 'Rosalie's not a kid any more. She's a young lady who strikes me as having a mind of her own.'

'I wish you'd come with us, Jenna. It would

'make all the difference.'

'How can I?' She looked fondly at her boisterous twin boys, happily emptying the contents of the cutlery drawer on the floor and enjoying the clatter. 'Who'd be willing to mind these two, even for one night? They get into everything.'

But Joe would not be diverted from his plan and thought he had found just the right event to break the ice. He bought tickets in advance, intriguing the boys by keeping it as a surprise. Sensing conspiracy, Rosalie tried to wriggle out of it at the last minute but Hannah wouldn't hear of it and pushed her into the passenger seat of Joe's old station wagon, telling her to 'live dangerously' for once. On the way to collect the boys, she tried to get Joe to tell her where they were going but he just smiled secretively, refusing to be drawn.

In clean clothes, freshly showered and smelling of a medicated soap, the boys piled into the back seat of Joe's wagon, scarcely acknowledging Rosalie. If Joe had hoped the young people would be excited enough to make conversation, he was disappointed. The boys were too shy and inhibited to say anything to Rosalie, who was equally unimpressed. After the initial introductions, she largely ignored them, staring out of the window at the boring scenery of the freeway — a seemingly endless ribbon of road, edged with grasses and stunted trees. Seeing this complete lack of interest on both sides, Joe had to admit that his wife had been right; no lasting friendships were going to be forged here tonight.

It was dusk by the time they reached their destination and it was Rosalie who first spotted the big top looming ahead of them, gaily painted in red and white stripes and with multi-coloured bunting fluttering in the breeze. Just catching sight of it brought all her worst memories flooding back. Long buried memories that she would rather forget.

'Oh, no,' she muttered, biting her lip. 'You're not taking us to a circus, Joe?'

'Rosalie, come on!' Realizing his careful planning wasn't appreciated, Joe's patience was finally exhausted. 'Don't tell me you have a hang-up about circuses? There's no cruelty these days. And they don't keep wild animals either because I checked. Just some horses for the bare-backed riders and little dogs.'

Rosalie couldn't answer him because her chest felt so tight she could scarcely breathe. Among the circus vehicles, she had seen vans depicting prancing horses with feathered head-dresses, but surely all circus ponies wore things like that? It was already too late to turn around — they were in a line of traffic being flagged into a nearby field to join a line of parked cars.

'This is so cool, Joe.' No longer shy, the older cousin — whose name Rosalie had already forgotten — became animated for the first time that night. 'We've never been to a circus before.'

Rosalie closed her eyes and tried to compose herself. Her legs were shaking and she wondered if she'd have the strength to get out of the car. Somehow she managed to follow the others as they made their way towards the big top where a clown was collecting tickets at the door.

'Welcome!' he was saying to everyone. 'Welcome to Tarquin's Travelling Circus!'

Once again in her memory, she was reliving that last terrible night. She could almost smell those fiery rings, experience yet again the shock of her beloved pony's fall and the horror of Edmond's scorched head. Everything was conspiring to bring it all back to her, even the scent of crushed grass underfoot, the animal odours and the frantic barking of little dogs. Added to that were the all too human smells of sweat and greasepaint, intensified by the air of excitement and anticipation from the audience moving in to take their seats inside the big top. Obviously, this old-fashioned entertainment was popular as ever but how could she tell her companions of the darker side of the circus world; the jealousy and spite that could exist just beneath the surface of the glittering spangles, the brightest smiles?

It's going to be all right, she kept repeating to herself like a mantra. This is only a little local circus. Nothing more. The circus people you know are in Italy on the other side of the world. It would be far too much of a coincidence for them to be here.

'Welcome!' the clown was spruiking as he collected the tickets. 'Welcome to Tarquin and Cleo's Travelling Circus — coming to you all the way from Italy for the Australian summer. Roll up! Roll up! Good tickets still available — tell your friends! Don't miss this rare and unique event!'

Please, Rosalie was praying silently now. Please — if there is a God — don't let me see anyone that I know. Taller than most girls, she slouched, trying to make herself inconspicuous but it was no use.

'Rosalie!' The clown startled her by recognizing her and shouting her name over the heads of the people in front of him, making her freeze and look up. 'Yes, I thought it was you! What a lovely surprise.' He clicked his fingers for another clown to take over his ticket collecting as he jumped down from his perch to draw Rosalie and her companions to one side.

'I'm sorry,' she started to say. 'You've made a mistake. I'm not the person you — '

'Oh yes, she is!' The older cousin shoved her quite roughly, finding his voice at last; he wasn't going to miss the chance of meeting a circus performer. 'Her name *is* Rosalie and she's with us.' He grinned at the clown who pulled off his red nose and grinned back, allowing Rosalie to recognize him as Luca.

'Rosie, I'm so pleased to see you again — and all in one piece. I had the most awful feeling when you left with Drago that day. Cassia wasn't too happy about it, either.'

She could see there was no point in pretending any longer so she sighed and stepped into a hug with Luca. 'It's good to see you too, Luca. And still on the road with Cleo and Cassia? That is a surprise.'

'Not when I tell you I'm married to Cassia, although it's Tarquin and Cleo who run the show. Tarquin's an Australian — he's the money these days.'

Rosalie realized then that Joe was watching this exchange, looking puzzled. 'You know these circus people, Rosalie? They're friends of yours?'

'And relatives, too. But it's a long story

— not always a happy one.'

Inside the tent, the circus band was striking up, signalling the show was about to begin.

'I have to go, folks,' Luca continued to speak in English so that Joe and the boys would understand. 'I'm needed to start the show. But please, don't disappear on me, will you? I know Cassia will want to see you afterwards. She feels guilty she didn't stand up for you more and has often wondered what happened to you. Look, I know where you're sitting. I'll come and collect you after the show.'

'We'd love to, Luca, but maybe not this time. We have a long journey ahead of us afterwards and I don't think — '

'Don't worry — we'll wait.' It was the elder cousin who spoke, ignoring Rosalie's frown and shake of the head. He was forming an idea to ask Luca if they had any jobs going. More fun than the work they were doing at present, digging holes to plant fruit trees. Joe said nothing, just as intrigued as the boys to learn more about these exotic people from Rosalie's past.

* * *

To Rosalie, the show was just like old times, although the acrobats and trapeze artistes were new. There had been little change to Cleo and Cassia's routines although their ponies were unfamiliar — probably purchased or borrowed from someone here. Cleo looked even more muscular and hatchet-faced than ever and Rosalie felt uncomfortable to be seated so close to her; they had never been friends. Luca was still in charge of the clowns who were gentler and less boisterous than the rough young men of her father's day. There was a new ringmaster too, probably Tarquin, a heavy-set bear of a man who didn't cut such an elegant figure as Drago.

Finally, as all the performers crowded into the ring and the band struck up the music for the grand finale, she made one last attempt to get Joe and the boys to leave. They refused to move, determined to see the show to the very end. In any case, even as the last performers were leaving the ring, Luca was there, ushering them towards a different exit at the rear of the tent.

He led them among the maze of caravans belonging to the circus folk and flung open the door of the spacious mobile home that he shared with Cassia. Cassia herself was already there, looking younger and prettier than Rosalie remembered. Marriage clearly agreed with her; she had added a few pounds in weight and it suited her, softening features that had once been as sharp as her sister's. As yet there was no sign of Cleo and she began to feel less tense, breathing a little easier.

'Rosalie.' Cassia pulled her into a firm embrace, surrounding them with the rather cloying, exotic perfume she favoured. She spoke English now out of politeness to their other visitors. 'How lovely to see you — and quite the young lady now. What a small world it turns out to be. But what are you doing in Melbourne? This is the last place we expected to find you.'

'It's such a long story,' Rosalie murmured. 'I don't really know where to begin.'

'And this young man is your husband?' Cassia smiled at Joe, causing the cousins to snigger together.

'No, no, we are all just friends — Joe's married already. We just work together.' Rosalie spoke quickly to cover her embarrassment. 'Cassia, I'm sorry but I can't relax until I know. My father's not here with you, is he? You have a new ringmaster.'

Cassia clapped her hands over her mouth. 'Oh my God! It was over three years ago now. Did you really not hear what happened to Drago?'

Rosalie shook her head, having a sinking feeling. She had always known her grandfather was a man who kept many secrets and she had found it odd that he never mentioned Drago after he left. At the time she had thought it better not to ask.

'Rosalie, your father died in Sicily soon after you got there. He lost control of the camper van and drove it off a cliff. Luca and I were afraid you were with him but they said only Drago's body was found in the wreckage. Cleo wouldn't let anyone go to his funeral. I think she let Angelo pay. As you were there at the time, we thought you must know. I'm so sorry, Rosalie.'

'It's OK. Don't be. We never had much of a relationship, anyway.' She felt slightly ashamed that the only emotion she felt was relief that Drago was no longer there to torment her.

Before anyone could say anything more, the caravan door was flung open to admit Cleo, as spiteful and aggressive as Rosalie remembered her. She was wearing a red silk dressing gown that was hardly decent and her long, dark hair was still wet from a recent shower. Drops of water flew from it as she tossed it around, wasting no time in confronting Rosalie.

Intending all those present to understand her, she spoke in English that was surprisingly good. Edmond must have been coaching her, too.

'So it's true. The bad penny has turned up

to haunt us. The source of all our woes. I knew it would have to happen sooner or later. You have a lot of explaining to do, missy.'

'Now just a minute.' Having taken an instant dislike to Cleo, Joe thought it was time to step in and take charge. After all, he was partly responsible for this drama, dragging Rosalie to the circus when she'd been so against it. 'I don't know who you people are to Rosalie but you've given her more than one unpleasant surprise tonight and it's enough. We have a long journey ahead of us and we need to leave — now. Working with racehorses means that we keep early hours.'

'So the lovely Rosalie works with race-horses now?' Cleo snapped back. 'Come up in the world, hasn't she? Our little skivvy.'

'There's no need to be nasty, Cleo,' Cassia said. 'She doesn't deserve it.'

'No?' She glared around at Joe and the two boys. 'You people should heed my warning and look out for yourselves. Folks have a habit of dying around Rosalie. Proper jinx, she is. And not just people — horses, too!' Hearing Joe's quick, indrawn breath, she was encouraged to go on. 'She won't have told you the half of it. My lovely Edmond was the first to die. If she hadn't come to us with that wretched Shetland pony, he might still be alive.'

'Cleo, please stop.' Cassia felt bound to intervene. 'You're distorting the facts. Rosalie didn't do anything. If you must blame someone, blame Drago.'

'But he was the next one to die in her company, wasn't he? Heed the gypsy's warning, people. I'm telling you — Rosalie is the angel of death.'

'Oh, stop it, sis. Only you could create a drama out of a simple road accident.'

'There's nothing simple about driving off a cliff. And that wasn't the end of it, either. There's her grandfather or uncle, whatever — who ended up in a bloodbath in his study and with most of his servants dead, too.'

'Everyone knows it was a power struggle between rival Mafia barons — that's what the papers said.'

'And you believe everything you read in the papers, Cassia?' Cleo sneered.

'I'm sorry, Rosalie,' Luca spoke in a low voice. 'If I'd known this would happen, I wouldn't have brought you here. Cleo gets into these rages sometimes — she used to take drugs until Tarquin put a stop to it. Sometimes we wonder if she's in her right mind.'

'And you can shut up as well, Luca!' Cleo turned on him. 'Stop talking about me as if I'm not here.'

Joe and the two boys stood huddled together as if frozen with shock. Suddenly, the little living room of the van seemed too small for so many people.

'It's time for us to leave,' Joe said in the silence that followed.

'Yes, please,' Rosalie said, shocked herself by all these unjust accusations. But now she thought about it, she could see it was all true. It was coincidental of course but those people had all died when she was around. She gave mute thanks to a God she didn't believe in that Cleo wouldn't know about Mary. Although Joe's thoughtful expression told her that particular death was now on his mind.

'And I'm not done yet.' Cleo stood in front of the door, hindering their departure. 'If nothing else, Rosalie is a Mafia granddaughter. What about Mary Browne, missy? Aha! You didn't expect me to know about that one, did you? But I thought I recognized you on television — you weren't there for more than a split second but I saw you all right — standing next to the society bride gunned down on her wedding day. I don't even have to ask — I'm sure it was you.'

Luca had heard enough and, shaking his head, manhandled Cleo out of the way, allowing their visitors to escape.

'Please don't believe any of this,' he

whispered to Joe as they passed. 'It's all nonsense — along with the so-called gypsy heritage. Once Cleo gets a bee in her bonnet, she goes crazy.'

★　★　★

Nobody spoke until they reached the car and climbed gratefully inside. Joe was especially thoughtful, mentally sifting everything. Cleo was obviously crazy but he couldn't help feeling there might be a seed of truth in her mad tirade. Only the elder cousin had something to say.

'Phew,' he said, waving his hand in front of his face as if dispersing a bad smell. 'What a horrid old woman. I was going to ask Luca if they had any jobs going. Don't think I'll bother now.'

Somehow this lightened the mood, making everyone laugh. But for Rosalie, the laughter didn't last for long.

Joe didn't have much to say until the two boys had been dropped off at the fruit farm; his efforts at match-making had not been a success.

'Thanks, pal.' The older boy gave Joe a friendly punch to the shoulder. 'That circus was amazing. Even if meeting the circus folk didn't turn out quite as I expected.' He gave a theatrical shudder. The younger cousin nodded, agreeing with his brother as usual.

With the boys gone, Rosalie waited for Joe to raise the queries that must be seething in his mind but instead of talking, he drove up to a big service station with a diner where he took her inside and bought a large cup of strong coffee and a doughnut for each of them. Only then did he seat himself opposite, leaving her no way of escaping his inquisition.

'So,' he smiled. 'My wife was right — as always. You're not about to fall madly in love with one of her cousins.'

Rosalie shifted in her seat. 'I'm afraid not. Although I'm sure they're both very nice.'

Joe laughed shortly. 'Very nice boys they are not. They didn't say half a word to you all night.'

'Joe,' she said, after taking a thoughtful sip of her coffee, 'you didn't bring me here to ask how I felt about Jenna's cousins.'

'No. No, I didn't.'

'So I'll make it easy. You want to know all about those circus people who seem to know me so well. And if there's any truth in what Cleo said.'

'I'm sure there isn't. You don't seem at all like the angel of death to me,' he was quick to reassure her. 'But I do know the boss and how trusting he can be. And those Mafia connections she mentioned are a bit worrying, after what happened to Mary. So if there remains some trouble in your life — something you haven't mentioned to Leo that might still come to his door — I want you to tell me about it now.'

'Honestly, Joe, Leo already knows all there is to know about me. I've nothing to hide. But there's no reason you shouldn't know the whole story, too.'

'And I twigged something else — you're not related to him at all, are you?'

She sat back and smiled. 'When did you work that one out?'

He just smiled in return, shaking his head.

'I used to think Cleo and Cassia were my aunts because my father, Drago, was their stepbrother — are you with me so far? But after that it starts to get complicated.'

Joe listened, spellbound, as she told him the story of her life, leaving nothing out — she even told him how her grandfather had been trying to marry her off at sixteen and how he had been brutally murdered in his own home. Hearing all this, Joe reacted only with a slight widening of the eyes as he waited to hear more. She concluded with how she met Leo on the ferry and how he had helped her so generously, allowing her a place in his life.

'He was there for me, Joe, when I needed it most. My very own knight in shining armour. So why should you be surprised that I fell in love with him?'

'You're not in love with him, Rosalie. He's old enough to be your father.'

'I've been totally honest with you, Joe. Don't presume to tell me how I feel.'

'OK. But what about Mary? You saw how he adored her. He may never feel the same about anyone else.'

Rosalie's eyes filled with unshed tears. 'Do you think I don't know that? You think I *choose* to feel this way? It's not comfortable at all, believe me.'

And there Joe had to leave it. Later that night when he climbed into bed with Jenna, trying not to wake her, she opened one sleepy eye, regarding him.

'How'd it go, then? The romance of the century? Are we to hear wedding bells soon?' she asked until Joe snorted, making her smile. 'Told you so.'

She turned over, hoping to get back to sleep.

'I'm done playing Cupid, I tell you,' he muttered, knowing he'd feel like rubbish when it was time to get up.

'Good,' she said, snuggling into her pillows.

12

That night Rosalie couldn't sleep. Her mind kept returning to Cleo and those bitter accusations. Like it or not, there was some truth in them. Terrible things did seem to happen when she was around.

She pounded her pillow and tried to clear her mind of these morbid thoughts but it was no use, she kept hearing Cleo's accusing voice in her mind — 'she's a jinx — the angel of death'.

At last, she fell into an exhausted sleep, although she felt scarcely rested at all when the alarm intruded on her troubled dreams to tell her it was time to get up and go to work at the stables. In the bright light of a hopeful early morning, she was able to set her nightmares aside. It would be crazy to let herself believe what Cleo had said. It wasn't her fault if trouble followed her because of Drago and his bad decisions, or her grandfather with his dubious underworld connections. She reminded herself that Leo himself had experienced more than enough trouble because of his own Sicilian relatives. The dark shadows hadn't been reaching out only towards herself.

At the stables, Joe wasn't at all his usual, cheerful self and Rosalie hoped it was just because he was tired and not because he was starting to believe what Cleo had said. Fortunately, no horses were due at the track this day and Nikki was there to help with the morning exercise so that she and Leo were able to go home for an earlier breakfast than usual. Hannah, of course, was delighted to see them do justice to a hearty meal, dishing up plates of fresh mushrooms and sausages as well as the inevitable bacon and eggs.

When the post arrived, Leo frowned when he saw he had a letter from Italy, almost afraid to open it in case it was a note containing more threats from his uncle. If Alberto could bear a grudge for so many years, it was unlikely that he would be satisfied with the death of Mary — he would continue his campaign of terror. But the letter was not from the uncle who had driven him so unceremoniously from his door; it was from a girl by the name of Guida, introducing herself as his cousin. The letter was in Italian of course and he was, at first, unwilling to let Rosalie translate it for fear of what it might contain as his own grasp of Italian wasn't that good.

'Oh, give it to me, Leo,' she said. 'Whatever

it has to say — good or bad — at least we'll be forewarned.'

She scanned it quickly and then smiled, reassuring him. 'No — we can relax. I promise — it's nothing but good news.'

Greetings Leo, she translated,

I have news that will be as much a relief to you as it is to us. My father — Alberto Marino — died of a stroke last week, releasing my mother and I from the many years we spent under his bullying control and disparagement. He wanted a son but there was always only me and he blamed my mother constantly for this omission. Now he is gone at last, I hope to bring some joy into the autumn of her life. Wanting to keep me close as an unpaid servant, my father never allowed me to marry but now I have hopes that it won't be too late for that.

We both knew what he planned for your wedding day — he boasted of it — but there was nothing we could do to prevent it, not even to warn you. I make haste to tell you that you have nothing to fear from him now that he's gone and most of his henchmen too. We feel that a huge weight has been lifted from our shoulders and hope that in time, you will, too. We are so desperately sorry for my father's cruel actions and hope you'll be able to put your tragedy behind you and make a new life for yourself as we now hope to do.

In sorrow for your loss, Guida Marino.

PS My mother endorses my words and says she will pray for you, too.

'Well,' Hannah said at last. 'It's not in my nature to dance on anyone's grave but if anyone deserves to fry in hell it should be that wicked man.'

Leo cleared his throat, speaking gently. 'Nothing can bring Mary back — I've said so before — but it was kind of Guida to write with this news, setting my mind at rest.'

'What a life they must have had with him,' Hannah said softly and Leo knew she would be thinking of her own abusive husband.

Also in Leo's post was a package containing papers advertising a big horse sale to take place in Auckland, New Zealand, in a few weeks' time; a combined sale of both breeding stock and animals ready for training.

'Sounds interesting. I think I might go this time,' Leo said, looking less careworn that he had in months. 'We don't have a superstar aside from Romeo's Secret. I might even buy two colts, if they're promising enough.'

'Let me go with you, Leo,' Rosalie said, eyes shining. 'I used to go to the horse sales with Uncle Carlo when I was a teenager. Even at that early age, he trusted me to pick out a good horse better than he did.'

'No, I don't think so, Rosalie,' Leo said shortly, refusing to meet her gaze.

'Oh, why not? I've been living here for more than three years now and never been anywhere. Not even for a holiday.'

'It isn't a holiday,' he said dismissively. 'This is important — it's work.'

'Yes. Work I've just told you I'm good at, so why can't I go?'

'Yes, why not take the girl, Leo?' Hannah chipped in. 'Last year was terrible with — well with everything.' She didn't want to bring him down by reminding him of Mary. 'Why not take Rosie with you? She works harder than most of the lads and it's time she had a break.'

'All right. All right, she can have one!' Leo's temper snapped. 'She can go to the Gold Coast or further north if she wants, to take a look at the reef. I'll pay. But she won't be going to New Zealand with me.'

'I think Jenna said she and Joe went to Bali once,' Rosalie said, looking thoughtful.

'And you're not going there, either,' Leo

258

said, trying to put an end to the conversation.

Exasperated, Hannah waved a tea towel at him. 'Then where *can* she go?'

'I've just told you. Anywhere she likes within Australia. It's just not possible for her to travel overseas.'

'Why not?' Rosalie's own temper rose, Leo's attitude starting to annoy her. 'I'm not a child any more and I can look after myself, if I need to. Remember those Kiwi guys who came through a few months ago at the time of the carnival? I made quite an impression — they told me to keep in touch and said I'd have a job waiting for me in New Zealand any time.'

'The cheek of those two. Coming over here and trying to pinch my staff. I'll have a word with those guys when I see them again.'

'At the time they probably didn't mean it and neither did I. But if I do turn up on their doorstep, they'll have to give me a job.'

Leo paused to take a deep breath, knowing that what he had to say next would upset her. 'Look Rosalie, I know you won't want to hear this but you can't go overseas. Not on a forged passport.'

'Why not? Nobody said anything when we came in.'

'Because it was the only way to get you into the country without a fuss. And we were lucky that day. The Customs people were busy congratulating themselves on a drug bust and it was the early hours of the morning.'

'So? We can go out in the early hours of the morning again.'

'I'm sorry but we're not risking it. If you're caught travelling on a forged passport, you could face detention or worse. If you want a holiday, go to Queensland or even WA but please, don't try to go overseas on that passport.'

'But it looks exactly the same as yours. How can they tell it's a forgery?'

Leo sighed. 'I wasn't going to mention it until all this came up but I had a phone call last week from my friend, Harry, at the Australian Embassy in Rome.'

'Oh?'

'He says there's a fuss blown up about forged Australian passports — Delbert Cromwell must've got careless and over-confident, I suppose. Harry's waiting to see if they track the man down and so far so good — our names haven't come into it — but he's keeping a close watch and he'll keep me posted.'

'I don't believe you.' Rosalie narrowed her eyes at him. 'Why should this happen just now while we're having this argument? How do I know you're not making it up to stop me from going to New Zealand?'

He shrugged. 'You'll have to take my word for it.'

'Ha!' Rosalie said, pushing back her chair and making it screech on the flagstones before flouncing out of the kitchen door.

* * *

When they met for an early supper downstairs in the kitchen some time later, Rosalie looked mutinous and picked at her food, still not speaking to Leo. The awkward silence continued until Hannah was unable to stand the tension in the room any longer and she switched on the small television she kept for company in the kitchen, hoping to lighten the mood.

She did so just in time to catch an item of breaking news. *Forged Australian passport scandal in Rome!* the headlines screamed. *Illegal immigrants entering Oz through the back door!* And then: *Embassy officials to be investigated — how much did they really know?*

'Now perhaps you'll believe me,' Leo said to Rosalie who had been anxiously watching it, biting her lips.

'What does this mean?' Hannah said,

261

realizing the tension between Leo and Rosalie had increased. 'And how does it affect you and Rosie?' The news broadcast shifted to local sporting events so she turned it off, folding her arms and turning to face them. 'What haven't you told me?'

'Oh, Hannah.' Leo sat back and sighed. 'There's so much that really I don't know where to start.'

'At the beginning, Leo. From the time you came home from Italy with this young girl you said was your niece or your cousin. Come to think of it, you've never told me exactly how you're related.'

'Because we're not,' Leo said.

Then he told Hannah everything, from that first meeting on the ferry and Rosalie's desperate need to get away from the gangsters who had murdered her grandfather. When he finished, Hannah sat down and sighed, shaking her head.

'Don't do things by halves, do you, Leo?' she said. 'You must think a lot of this girl to take so many risks for her.'

Rosalie glanced at Leo, realizing this must be true; something that hadn't occurred to her until now.

'So, what shall we do?' Hannah said, ever practical. 'Sit tight and wait to see if the Feds swing by to arrest her? You do understand you could be in trouble yourself for assisting her?'

'No need to panic just yet,' Leo said. 'If we keep our cool and behave as if everything's normal maybe it will pass us by.'

'And if not? If Rosalie is investigated?' Hannah said. Leo had never seen her so serious. 'I know something of these things, Leo. I was a young girl in Berlin before the wall came down. Terrible times. People with or without proper papers could disappear in the middle of the night.'

'This is Australia, Hannah,' Leo said. 'That doesn't happen here.'

'Don't get me started. There are detention camps here where the press aren't allowed to go. Do you want to see Rosalie trapped there? If she comes to the attention of the authorities, they will ask for her birth certificate — they'll want to know who her parents are, exactly when they came to Australia and where she was born.'

'But why should they investigate her? She's already been here for three years.'

'Because this business of the false passports is coming to their attention only now. Tell me exactly how Rosalie's passport was made.'

'The forgery guy, he — um — borrowed mine.'

'And did you really think he'd use it just

once to create one for Rosalie? Oh, Leo! He must have thought all his Christmases had come at once. A genuine modern Australian passport that he could copy as many times as he liked.'

Leo groaned, closing his eyes.

'So it's no use burying our heads in the sand, hoping it all goes away,' Hannah went on to say. 'We need Plan B and it had better be a good one. Let's sleep on it and see what we come up with in the morning.'

Leo came up with a Plan B although he knew the conventionally minded Hannah would think it extreme. For this reason he decided to run it past Rosalie first. The idea came to him as he watched her handling the horses and he wondered why he hadn't thought of it before. She had devoted herself to the stables and his horses so seamlessly, he had been taking her for granted for too long. But now he had the chance to do something for her in return. With Mary gone, leaving such a huge gap in his life, he no longer cared about his own future. He thought he had found the perfect solution to Rosalie's problem — a way to be sure of keeping her safe. And he was so pleased with it, he couldn't wait to share the idea.

As usual, she was last to leave the stables, so he captured her as she was saying a last goodnight to Beppo before she went back to the house. He expected her to be relieved if not entirely pleased with his solution. Rage had not been on the list.

Breathing heavily, she drew herself up to her full height to confront him, two spots of colour blooming on her cheekbones, contrasting badly with her reddish gold hair.

'Leo, no! What are you thinking? Of course I can't marry you!' Her voice was trembling with both anger and shock.

'Oh, I know. I'm too old for you, of course — I understand that. But please listen to me for a moment because it won't be the way that you think.'

'Then what way is it going to be? Don't you know I'm a jinx? A bad luck charm? People have a habit of dying around me.'

'That's rubbish. Joe told me what happened at the circus and what that stupid woman said. I don't believe a word of it and neither should you.'

'Oh yes, everything's going to be fine — until something happens. But that's not my only reason for turning you down. You're still in love with Mary, aren't you?'

'What if I am? She's gone and I'll never see her again. Hard as that is, I have to accept it.'

'That doesn't mean your feelings have gone away. I was there, remember, on the day that you met. You looked like a man whose life-long dream had just walked into his life. Anyone could see you were made for each other. And now you insult me by asking me to be second choice.'

'But that's not what I'm asking — really I'm not. If only you'll get down from your high horse for a moment and listen to me.'

'Honestly, Leo.' She plonked herself down on a bale of straw nearby. 'This might be one of the times that I wish I drank.'

'There's a bottle of Irish whiskey in Joe's office.'

'I'm joking, you idiot.' She glared at him.

'Oh, right.' He looked at her warily. 'Can you hear what I have to say without flying off the handle or not?'

'All right,' she snapped. 'But don't expect my answer to be any different.'

'Let's get one thing straight from the beginning. I won't expect you to make love with me. You won't even have to share my bed.'

'Oh? And what sort of a marriage is that?'

'A marriage of convenience — for both of us. Married to me, no one can touch you and you'll no longer be an illegal immigrant.'

'OK. I get all of that. But I don't see what's in it for you.'

'Nothing — except the satisfaction of

knowing I've done my best to protect you. I have already lost the love of my life. I don't expect to meet another.'

Rosalie folded her arms and fixed him with a stern look. 'And what about the love of *my* life?'

He stared at her, taken aback. 'Oh, Rosalie, I didn't know you had one. I've never even seen you go out on a date.'

'What planet have you been living on? I have a laptop. People meet via the internet now.'

'Isn't that dangerous? I've heard of paedophiles hiding behind false identities to trap the unwary.'

'Well, I'm sure it happens and I might have been stupid enough to fall for such a thing once — I used to be very naïve — but that time I spent with the circus made me grow up fast.'

'OK. Who is this paragon you met on the internet? And when do I get to meet him?'

'You won't. Because I'm teasing you, Leo. No such person exists. But I'm not closing the door and saying it couldn't happen.'

Leo winced, shaking his head. 'Rosalie, you don't seem to realize we're in the midst of a bad situation here. I do wish you'd take it more seriously.'

'Oh, I do. I take it very seriously when

someone asks me to marry him. There's just one thing stopping me, Leo. You don't love me.'

'Not in that way, no. But I am very fond of you.'

She just smiled, shaking her head.

'If it helps you to accept the idea, I'll make a deal with you,' he said. 'I'll even get it drawn up like a contract. When you meet the person you really want to marry — as you most certainly will — I'll make it easy for you to divorce me.'

'Oh, goodie,' she said with little enthusiasm.

'But please, sweetheart, don't waste too much time thinking about it. Someone in Rome might be giving our names up, even as we speak. Think about it overnight and give me your answer in the morning.'

'I can give you my answer now.'

'Please don't be flippant about this and please don't just say no to me without thinking it over . . . '

'But I'm saying YES!' She sprang to her feet and hugged him. 'I'm going to be Mrs Leo Marino, and then all these stables will be mine.'

'Oh?' he said. 'I never realized you could be so mercenary.'

'You should be careful, Leo.' Her smile was

all mischief. 'You might find out that you don't really know me at all.'

* * *

When they announced it to Hannah over breakfast the next day, they could see she was far from enchanted with the idea although, for the time being, she kept her opinions to herself. She murmured half-hearted congratulations but they could see that this news had shocked her. But she waited until Rosalie left to go back to the stables, before airing her views to Leo.

'I hope to goodness you know what you're doing, Leo,' she said. 'I can see all this ending in heartbreak.'

'Well, Hannah, what else can I do?' He sat back and sighed. 'There's not one person left in the world to look out for her — and if she's sent back to Italy, she'll be like a displaced person — a refugee.'

'There has to be someone. What about those two from the circus — Luca and Cassia, wasn't it? She spoke quite warmly about them.'

'Itinerant showmen who can scarcely keep body and soul together themselves? I don't think so.'

'I'm just trying to find another solution

that isn't as drastic as marriage.'

'Don't think I haven't tried. It's the only thing I can think of to keep her safe.'

Hannah shook her head as she pushed a fresh cup of coffee before him and he smiled his thanks.

'But there's something else, Leo. Something you haven't thought of and never expected. Why d'you think Rosie is so willing to let you do this for her?'

'Not so willing to start with, I can tell you. She was quite angry with me at first for suggesting it. Until she thought about it for a while and the mercenary side of her nature kicked in.'

'Mercenary?' Hannah stared at him in astonishment. 'If that's what you think, you don't know her at all. That girl doesn't have a mercenary bone in her body. Why d'you think she works like a dog in your stables? For the miserable wages you pay her?'

'Fair go. I wouldn't say they were *that* miserable.'

'Don't change the subject. Rosalie works hard because she's in love with you, Leo — and has been for years.'

'Oh, surely not. She's just a — '

'Don't you dare say she's just a kid. Maybe she was when you brought her from Italy but she's a young woman now. She's been like a daughter to me and I've watched her grow up. She is genuinely in love with you and that's why she's agreed to this marriage.'

'Honestly, Hannah, I had no idea. What am I going to do?'

'The only thing you can do now. Fulfil your promise to marry the girl and do your best to make her happy.'

★   ★   ★

Rosalie received a similar grilling when she confided this latest news to Joe. She wanted to tell him first before the gossip-mongers had it all over the stables. She was grooming Beppo at the time, wanting something to do with her hands. But he rounded on her before she had the chance to explain about the fake passport and the consequent need for haste.

'Next week, Rosie? You say you're going to marry the man next week? Have you lost your senses?' He appeared to be one step away from shaking her. 'Leo doesn't know what he's doing — he's still out of his mind with grief over Mary. And, as I said before, he's old enough to be your father.'

'Well, he isn't my father, is he? Joe, listen to me. It means I can have what I want and I really don't care how I get it. This is something I've longed for and never expected to happen. So I'll take any crumbs from his table — the smallest part of him that he's willing to share.'

Joe shook his head. 'Be careful what you wish for, Rosie.'

'Oh, shut up. You've always known how I feel and I expected you of all people to be happy for me. I'm sure Jenna will. She knew better than to try and fix me up with her idiot cousins like you did.'

'All right — that was a mistake. I admitted it at the time. But I'll still do my best to stop you making a worse one.'

'Why? Why is everyone so certain that it's a mistake?'

'Aha, so I'm not the only one. I'll bet Hannah doesn't think so much of it, either.' He tried to hold Rosalie's gaze but she turned her back on him, hiding her face in Beppo's luxuriant mane. 'I thought not.'

13

Looking at the computer in his study, Leo scrolled down his emails, wondering which ones to answer or ignore. Although he had done his best to contain it, the news of his forthcoming marriage to his stable girl — scandalously reported to be some sort of relative — had been leaked and now everyone seemed to have an opinion, feeling obliged to offer him their advice. Some of the more offensive comments had come from people he hardly knew, condemning Rosalie as a gold digger and himself for being such an easy mark. He had messages from Mary's relatives, too, accusing him of being faithless and disrespectful by rushing into another marriage so soon after her death. He wasn't even sure how the news had come out, although he suspected Jenna who loved to gossip and couldn't keep her mouth shut about anything. He felt like writing just one word in capital letters and sending it to all of them — M Y O B!

Only Hannah and Joe knew of the real circumstances behind this hastily arranged wedding and he had no intention of satisfying anyone else's curiosity. To draw least attention, the ceremony would be performed by a marriage celebrant before a few witnesses in Hannah's rose garden and there was no thought of a honeymoon. In view of the circumstances, it wasn't appropriate and the last thing they needed was further attention from the media vultures.

While he was lost in his thoughts, wishing the news had been kept closer to home, Hannah poked her head around the door, noting his wretched expression. 'Stop reading those emails, Leo, if you know what's good for you. It'll be a nine day wonder to most people and once you're married and settled, they'll turn their attention to someone else.'

Leo groaned. 'I hope you're right, Hannah. I've felt like a goldfish in a bowl, ever since this whole thing started.'

'Sorry to intrude when I know you're so busy, but there's someone downstairs that I think you should see. I've put him in the sitting room and given him coffee.'

'Oh, Hannah, why? I don't want to see anyone. I'm so sick of all their 'well-meaning' advice. If I hear one more person say 'it's for your own good', I'll punch his lights out.'

'It's only because they don't know all the facts.'

'Right. But if people had to suffer the

consequences of their unwanted advice, they might not offer it so freely. So tell me, who's the latest idiot with an opinion who's waiting for me downstairs?'

'Come down and see for yourself. I think you'll want to hear what this man has to say.'

'I doubt it,' Leo muttered, bristling with temper as he followed her down the stairs and headed for the sitting room, meaning his unexpected visitor to have a very short stay. But when the visitor jumped to his feet and greeted him pleasantly, he was at once disarmed, although he wasn't sure why.

'I hope I haven't called at a bad time,' the visitor said. 'I'm Mary's older brother — Michael Browne.'

'Oh, right. The mysterious war correspondent. She did mention you briefly. Said you couldn't come to the wedding because you were away overseas.' He cleared his throat, still finding it hard to mention Mary by name. This older brother wasn't really like her at all but there were enough subtle similarities to renew Leo's grief.

'And you didn't even make it to her funeral.' He couldn't hold back the reproach.

'My time isn't really my own. And I wouldn't have been welcome anyway. I'm the black sheep of the family, you see. But never mind that. I'm here today for one reason only

— to let you know there was a lot more to our sainted Mary than first met the eye.'

Leo sprang to his feet. 'Now, that's enough. Your sister is dead and buried. If there was bad blood between you, I don't want to know and I won't listen to anything that might tarnish her spotless reputation.'

'There you go, you see. Saint Mary. I could tell you she was a good actress but you probably wouldn't believe me. It was her protection against the less savoury aspects of life.'

'You can leave right now, Mr Browne,' Leo said, moving towards the door. 'We have nothing more to say to each other.'

'Look, Leo — I'm going to call you Leo whether you like it or not, after all, we were almost related. I came in the spirit of friendship and wouldn't be here unless it was really important. So please, won't you hear me out?'

'By all means. If you're willing to risk a bloodied nose. I won't let you ruin the memories I have of Mary.'

'Your memories are your own and no one can touch them now. But you should know that Mary was as much a victim of our father's ambition as I was. And do sit down again, please. You're making me nervous.'

Leo once more lowered himself into a

chair. 'Go on, then.'

'At risk of getting a punch in the face at the outset, I must ask you a very personal question — did you ever come close to sleeping with Mary?'

'You're right, it is personal and impertinent but I'll answer you anyway. No, there was no intimacy between us. She always said she wanted to wait until after the wedding.'

'I'm sure. And you'd have been lucky if it had taken place even then.'

'Why, you . . . '

'Whoa! Don't shoot the messenger. Let me rewind a bit and start the story from a different angle. I'll tell you why I'm *persona non grata* in our family. Dad cut me off without even the proverbial shilling when he found out I was gay. He couldn't accept that he had a son who liked dressing in silver and marching in the Gay Mardi Gras.'

'Having met Mr Browne, I can quite believe that. Not the most tolerant of men.'

'So he made Mary his heir instead and I was OK with that because I loved my sister. I was already a journalist and knew I'd be able to make my way on my own but she couldn't. She must have been around nineteen at the time but the real damage to Mary happened long before that.'

Leo had a sinking feeling, already aware

that the news wasn't going to be good. 'What damage? I'm not sure what you mean.'

'Did she ever tell you she went to a girls' boarding school?'

'It never came up. We were both adults and our schooldays were long behind us.'

'Our mother was a perennial invalid — in and out of hospitals and nursing homes all the time — so Dad had several mistresses. Because he wanted to bring them to the house, he sent Mary and I away to boarding school. We both detested it and told him so many times but he didn't care. He didn't want us at home, seeing him with his women and cramping his lifestyle.'

Michael picked up his coffee and took a sip before going on.

'At Mary's school there was an end-of-year prom and some of the lads from a local grammar school were invited to come to the dance. It was a long-held tradition, so we were told. One of them took a fancy to Mary and they spent most of that evening together. Around supper time, she agreed to meet him outside in the garden, expecting to share a few innocent kisses. Instead, he punched her half senseless and dragged her into the bushes before tearing her dress from her body and raping her.'

'God, no! She never said anything.'

'And that wasn't all. When he'd finished, he called in his friends to take a share of the action. Mary was badly injured and torn, physically and emotionally. She had been a virgin, not even sixteen.'

'I hope those bastards suffered for it. Surely, her father must've — '

'No. I'm sorry to say our father wouldn't do anything. He said that what happened couldn't be mended and, since the boy came from a family of lawyers, Mary's name would be dragged through the mud if he tried to make a case of it. Her school principal was all too happy to have it hushed up. So was Mary. She was fragile enough without being subjected to cross-examination in court. Counselling might have helped but Dad wouldn't allow it. He wanted the whole thing swept under the carpet and forgotten — he said we should look on the bright side and be thankful she didn't get pregnant.'

'My poor girl.'

'Her hair turned white almost overnight and she wouldn't let any man close to her, not for years. Gained the reputation of being quite the ice princess.'

'Ice princess,' Leo repeated thoughtfully. 'Odd you should say that. When we were alone and I tried to kiss her, she would tremble and her lips tasted cold, almost frozen. But in company she was quite herself again, radiating generosity and warmth.'

'But she never allowed more than kisses, even though you were engaged?'

Leo shrugged. 'I didn't dwell on it. I thought she had strong religious principles, that's all.'

'Not Mary. She gave up believing in any just gods right after the rape. Did you ever see her go to church?'

'Not now I think of it. Except for our wedding and the necessary interviews with the vicar beforehand, no.'

'As I told you, she learned to be a good actress. She could make anyone believe she was a normal, warm-hearted woman — she certainly had you fooled. And do stop bunching your fists, you're making me nervous again.'

Leo sat back in his chair with a sigh. 'And there's more, isn't there? But now we've come this far, you might as well tell me everything.'

'I don't know how well you knew our father but he was a manipulative bastard. Came of being CEO of a big corporation, I suppose. He's a pathetic figure now, of course, lying in hospital waiting to die. Mary was the final pawn in his game. He was getting old and wanted to see her married, hopefully pregnant before he died. If she refused, he was threatening to cut her off and leave her with nothing. She believed him because he'd already done that to me.'

'Mary was a grown woman. She could have called his bluff and defied him.'

'You think? My sister was brought up to be a gracious hostess — to hold dinner parties and arrange flowers; an old-fashioned girl who'd have fared better in a much earlier era. She'd never done a stroke of work in her life. She had to submit to Dad's wishes and make the best of it. He cut me out of his life because of his prejudice but I know he loved Mary and he wasn't a cruel man. I think he did her a good turn when he chose you.'

'*He* chose me? But I always thought . . .'

'That the relationship you had with Mary happened spontaneously? Sorry to disappoint but it was well orchestrated from the beginning. And, as I told you before, she learned to be a good actress.'

'Except when it came to the prospect of making love,' Leo said thoughtfully. His mind was spinning, trying to absorb what he'd just heard. 'It's just too much to take in all at once, you've turned my whole world upside down,' he muttered as he stood up, intending to show Michael the door. After all these revelations, he needed some time alone and to think.

'I'm sorry.' Michael also rose to his feet. 'I can see that I've shocked you. But I didn't think you should marry again without knowing all the facts about Mary.'

'Thank you, Michael, for coming to see me and for your honesty. I didn't want to listen at first but now I'm glad that I did.'

'Good. I do wish you every happiness, Leo. Mary's life was blighted from the outset; she had terrible nightmares and never got over that night. Lovely as she seemed, it was all an illusion and she never stood a chance of living a normal life. Ultimately, as a wife, she would have disappointed you. And I couldn't let you go on thinking she was a saint and placing her on a pedestal for your new bride to live up to. That's all.'

'For obvious reasons, our wedding is going to be very small and discreet or I'd ask you to come.'

'Oh.' Michael looked down and smiled. 'Better not. That would pose even more questions, wouldn't it?' Taking this as his cue to leave, he shook Leo firmly by the hand. 'I might see you around, Leo. Or maybe not. The life of a war correspondent is never dull. I'm flying out to the Middle East tomorrow to report on a new uprising.

Not sure when I'll be back.'

'Safe journey then, Michael. And thank you again for taking the time to see me,' he said, accompanying his visitor to the door. He knew Hannah would be all agog to know why Mary's brother had come but he decided not to satisfy her curiosity. Mary was gone and the cruel things that had happened to her should stay buried, too.

He knew Hannah was unlikely to raise the subject of Michael's visit in front of Rosalie, hoping she might forget to do so at all but he had no such luck. Rosalie left the house that evening after supper, saying she was going to see Jenna and ask her advice about what she might wear for the wedding, allowing Hannah to seize her chance, coming straight to the point.

'That visitor you had today,' she said. 'Something about him reminded me of Mary. A relative, wasn't he?'

'Yes — he's her brother — Michael.'

'So why is he coming here now? What did he want?'

'Oh, nothing really — just to offer his condolences.' Leo was doing his best to avoid her penetrating gaze.

'Pull the other leg — it's got bells on,' Hannah said rudely. 'Just how stupid do you think I am? And you — you've been in a world of your own ever since he left. What did he have to say that upset you so?'

Leo sighed and blew out a long breath. 'If I tell you, Hannah, I want your promise that it will remain strictly between ourselves — and you certainly mustn't tell Rosie.'

'I can keep my trap shut, if I have to.' Hannah went to put the kettle on; something she always did in times of crisis. 'But if it's that bad, I'm not sure that I want to hear it.'

'Fine. OK,' Leo said, standing up and pushing his chair against the table.

'You stay right where you are. You can't pique a person's curiosity and then refuse to satisfy it.'

Leaving out the crucial details of what happened to Mary at boarding school, Leo told Hannah everything else, chiefly that his erstwhile fiancée had not really been in love with him but that she was a good actress coerced into marrying him by her father.

'Oh, Leo.' Hannah placed a comforting hand on his shoulder. 'So it was all a lie. Mary wasn't such a paragon, after all. I have to say there were times when I thought she really was too good to be true.'

'I didn't. I just counted my good fortune and never suspected a thing. I feel such a fool now.'

'You shouldn't. The poor girl is dead and

284

can't answer for anything. Her brother was right to come here. You and Rosie can start married life without a saint to look up to.'

'Oddly enough, that's what Michael said.'

14

Rosalie had no idea what she might wear to her wedding.

If Leo hadn't expressly ordered her not to wear white, she would have visited an opportunity shop and picked up a wedding dress there. Some of them were as fine as anything offered in bridal shops; she had marvelled at some of the elaborate dresses, nearly all as good as new, and so carelessly given away. Some, of course, were encrusted with jewels and completely over the top with crinoline skirts and an abundance of lace and bows but she had to wonder what bride could bear to part with the dress she had worn on that most important of days. Unless, later on, she had divorced the man she had vowed to cherish forever. Leo had promised to let her divorce him even before they had taken their vows.

But now she was faced with a dilemma. If she were to follow Leo's instructions and stay clear of white, what other colour would be acceptable instead? She wished she had just one of those beautiful, filmy dresses she had been forced to leave behind in her grandfather's villa. Some relative of Francesco's was probably jumping around in them now, crowing over her good fortune. And what about cream? Would Leo find that just as unacceptable as white? Finally, she went to Jenna to get some advice.

'Doesn't want to see you in white, eh? I suppose he's thinking of Mary,' Jenna said, rather tactlessly. 'And he's probably just as averse to cream.' She was pensive for a moment. 'Tell you what, I have friends with a vintage clothes shop in Chapel Street and I'm sure they'll have something suitable as well as unique.'

'Jenna, I don't know how to get around town because I've never been. And if I go on the train, I'll get lost for sure.'

'I suppose so.' Jenna bit her lip. 'Look, I haven't had a break from the boys for months. D'you think Hannah might be persuaded to take care of them? Just this once? Then I'd be able to drive you.'

'Oh, Jenna, that would be wonderful.' Rosalie hugged her. 'I can't thank you enough.'

'Don't thank me until we see if we can offload my little monsters on Hannah. If she has any sense, she'll say no.'

But Hannah agreed, only too happy for Rosalie to get a lift into town. And she was tactful enough not to mention her own misgivings about Jenna's taste that could sometimes be outrageous.

★　★　★

Waving goodbye to Hannah and the children, the girls were in high spirits, although Rosalie felt a pang of sadness when she remembered setting off in just the same way on those carefree shopping expeditions with Trizia. How naïve she had been in those days. But she forced those memories to the back of her mind. Today she was shopping for her wedding dress and this wasn't the time to remember all those sad things that couldn't be helped.

Although it was a fine, sunny day — or perhaps because of it — the vintage clothes shop belonging to Jenna's friends wasn't busy. Jenna was disappointed to find that the two boys who owned it were away at their farm but a pretty assistant, who looked a bit like Snow White, was happy to help them find Rosalie something amazing to wear.

'Pale green would be perfect with Rosalie's hair,' Jenna said. The hair that had been cut so severely by that hairdresser in Rome had grown and the luxuriant red-gold tresses had returned although, when she was working, she usually wore it pulled back in a ponytail, away from her face.

'Green with red hair is also a bit of a cliché,' the shop assistant said. 'But there's a 1930s dress in white satin the owners have just put out. I wish I was getting married myself because it's just perfect — beautifully cut and just the thing for a modern bride.'

'Oh, please, don't show me anything in white,' Rosalie said at once. 'That's the one thing Leo was clear about. Any colour other than white.'

'OK,' the girl said. 'There's another one that came from the same place — in pale blue. Would you like to see that?'

'No. Not pale blue, either,' Rosalie said, thinking of the pale blue dress Mary wore when she first came to the stables.

She sighed, wondering if this was going to be the pattern of her life from now on. A series of things she couldn't do and colours she couldn't wear in case Leo was reminded of Mary. Not for the first time, she was starting to have some serious doubts about what she was doing. Leo wasn't the only one to receive negative emails and postings on social media.

She realized both the other girls were looking at her, waiting for her to put forward her own suggestions.

'Midnight blue?' she offered. 'A fifties style maybe, with a full skirt that goes on forever . . . '

'Hang on — now you've said that, I think I have just the thing.' The shop assistant brightened with enthusiasm. 'A model frock that we think came from London or Paris.' And she left them, disappearing among a rack of clothes at the back of the shop.

'Midnight blue? You'll look like the mother of the bride in that.' Jenna frowned. 'You should aim to look like a fairy tale princess on your special day.'

'Leo's already had one fairy tale princess, remember?' Rosalie shrugged. 'It didn't end well.'

'Why are you marrying him, Rosalie? Love doesn't die overnight. And everyone knows that he's still in love with Mary,' Jenna said softly.

'I'm sure Joe must have told you what I said. I'll settle for whatever Leo can offer right now and hope that in time he'll love me as well.'

'And if not?'

'Let's wait and see shall we, Jenna?' Rosalie felt tears beginning to prick her eyes. For the first time she was wishing she'd taken her chances and come to Melbourne alone.

'Oh, I'm so sorry, love. Me and my big

mouth — I never meant to upset you.' Jenna made an attempt to heal the situation with a hug, although Rosalie remained stiff in her embrace, unable to respond.

Further awkwardness was prevented by the shop assistant arriving with exactly the sort of dress she had in mind. The fabric was heavy lace in a deep midnight blue, with a full skirt flowing from a fitted bodice embroidered with dark blue jewels and three-quarter sleeves to complete the fifties look. The waist was nipped in with a narrow belt made of the same fabric and the dress must have been treasured as it looked good as new. Tears forgotten, Rosalie smiled and went to try it on. Having been made for a tall model, it fitted her perfectly and both Jenna and the shop assistant gently applauded, giving it their approval.

A pair of silver pumps of the same vintage were found together with a small silver bag as she said she didn't intend to carry flowers.

'Well, it doesn't look anything like a wedding dress but I can't say it doesn't suit you,' Jenna said at last.

'Wear your hair up and it will make you look older, too,' the shop assistant said with a flash of intuition.

'Rosie, you have to look at this,' Jenna said, pointing to something in the showcase. It was a 1930s nightgown in silk and lace, still in its original box and never been worn. 'The perfect thing for you to wear on your wedding night.'

'I don't know, Jenna.' Rosalie showed little enthusiasm. 'It's probably too small for me, anyway.'

'I don't think so.' Jenna refused to give up so easily. 'It looks like it was made for a duchess and they ate cream cakes all the time. But if you're not going to buy it, I will. It's time I reminded Joe of the fun side of being a husband.'

The possibility of losing it made Rosalie buy it at once. It cost almost as much as the midnight-blue dress but she didn't care; a conventional wedding dress from a high street store would have cost a lot more.

While Rosalie continued her preparations for the wedding, Leo went to the sale in New Zealand alone. But, unable to make up his mind as well as being unused to the speed of the bidding, he came home empty-handed. Next time, he promised himself, he would travel with Rosalie and take advantage of her experience of horse fairs. He was surprised to find how much he was looking forward to it.

★　★　★

On the day of the wedding, the weather was beautiful; a sunny autumn day that wasn't too hot. Although the wedding guests had been kept to a minimum this time, the staff of the stables had turned up in force to see Rosalie as a bride. People had learned to love her and she had become a lot more popular than when she first arrived.

Although she insisted she wanted no attendants and the minimum of fuss, Nikki turned up with a posy of blue flowers chosen to match her dress. She also brought a few cornflowers to tuck into Rosalie's hair. She hadn't put it up as suggested but had chosen to wear it loose — a shining, flame-coloured halo around her face.

Leo was dressed in casual clothes this time — he didn't want to wear a suit or anything that might remind him of the calamity of his wedding to Mary. And there was another break from tradition as well. Since Rosalie had no one to give her away, she and Leo walked out of the house together to the rose garden where the marriage celebrant awaited them. They exchanged smiles, ready to make the brief vows they had composed for themselves. A murmur went through the assembled crowd from the stables; they had never realized that rangy, untidy Rosalie could make any claim to glamour or beauty but today she succeeded on both counts. Leo, meanwhile, was solemn and rather subdued. And, although he knew it was quite impossible with his uncle dead and safely six feet under in Italy, he couldn't help glancing around, fearing yet another attack. He could only hope no one else was aware of these troubling thoughts running through his mind.

The celebrant was an older woman with long, greying hair in a plait almost reaching her waist. Dressed all in white, she was still beautiful for her years. Her introduction to the ceremony was simple and to the point. She must surely know something of the circumstances bringing these two people together but it wasn't for her to show any criticism or opinion of her own.

Leo made his vows first, saying them simply and holding Rosalie's hands.

'Rosalie, my dearest girl, I can't offer you more than I can give at this time but I promise to do my best to make you happy. I will cherish you for the rest of my days and hope never to give you any cause for regret or to doubt me. I shall be yours for as long as you want me and I mean to honour these vows that I make today with all sincerity.' So saying, he kissed her hands, smiling into her eyes.

Although he was speaking softly for just

Rosalie and the celebrant to hear, most people standing nearby were quick to realize that among these sentiments there had been no mention of love and some of them glanced at each other with raised eyebrows.

Then Rosalie took her turn, speaking confidently.

'My dearest Leo, what can I say? I shall do my best to be the wife you deserve and, if I fail, it won't be for the want of trying. I've loved you so long I can't remember a time when I wasn't in love with you. I only hope that in time and with enough perseverance on my part, that you'll feel the same about me.

'I want only the best for you, Leo. I love you now and I always will.' She wanted to add something more but she felt tears threatening and her voice cracked, making it impossible for her to speak.

The celebrant realized it was time to step in. The rings were quickly exchanged and the ceremony was brought to a close with a kiss that Rosalie felt was more like that of a benevolent uncle than an emotional bridegroom. But for now she accepted it. She had what she wanted at last — she was married to Leo.

The marriage celebrant gave her a speculative look as if she had something more that she wanted to say and then decided against it.

'I can only wish you every happiness, my dear,' she said, resorting to cliché. 'And don't you disappoint her,' she said in an undertone to Leo before going back to her car and driving away.

Although Leo had tried to insist that there wasn't to be any wedding reception or fuss and they would all return to their usual routines straight away, he didn't reckon with Hannah who was determined to override his instructions. Joe and Jenna and most of the stable hands pretended they were on their way back to work, but they sneaked into the house instead where the diligent housekeeper had laid out a feast of epic proportions. All kinds of finger food surrounded a modest wedding cake on the dining room table. Nikki and Jenna had already decorated the room with streamers and flowers. And, except for Hannah, who went to the kitchen to meet them, everyone else stayed quiet when they heard the bride and groom come back to the house.

'We ought to have had a small party,' Rosalie said in a small voice. 'It feels like a bit of an anti-climax without one.'

'Least said — soonest mended,' Leo said. 'Who wants to throw a party when people have been so against the idea of us? I can't tell them I'm only doing it to keep you safe.'

'But it's my wedding day, Leo. And it should feel a bit more special than this.'

'You'll have another one, sweetheart. One day you'll meet the love of your life and you'll have your day out with all the trimmings, happy to kick the dust of old Leo off your — '

'Stop it! Just stop talking for one minute.' Beset with conflicting emotions, Rosalie wanted to burst into tears.

'Well now,' Hannah said brightly, having watched the exchange. 'This is my day for playing the fairy godmother. Cinderella, come with me. Because you *shall* go to the ball!'

'Hannah?' Leo said ominously. 'What have you done?'

Taking the arm of each, Hannah led the bride and reluctant groom towards the dining room, presently closed against them. 'Now, Joe!' she called out bravely.

The door of the dining room was flung upon and Hannah had to step back hastily as a cloud of confetti enveloped the bridal couple.

'Not in the house! I told you — not in the house!' Hannah cried out in vain.

'Don't worry, Hannah,' Nikki said. 'We'll all help you to clear it up.'

'Promises, promises,' Hannah said but she smiled.

Music was put on, everyone started to enjoy themselves and even Leo admitted that the party was a good idea. There was no formality and no speeches, just a happy bunch of people celebrating who knew one another well. And when the food was finally cleared away, Nikki made good her promise and swept up all the confetti, and the dining table and chairs were pushed to one side to make room for dancing.

All went well until, at the height of the festivities, Hannah signalled to Leo that there was a phone call and that he should take it. She didn't look happy.

'What now?' he said. 'Not another person telling me what a mistake I've just made?'

'It's your friend, Harry, calling from Rome.'

'Oh God, here we go,' he said. 'More bad news, I suppose. Don't want to spoil the party so I'll take it upstairs in my study.'

Leaving Rosalie happily dancing with Nikki, he bounded up the stairs and shut the door to his study before picking up the phone.

'Sorry to keep you, Harry,' he said. 'Bit of a shindig going on downstairs. So — give it to me straight. Have they caught up with

Delbert Cromwell yet? Just how bad is it going to be?'

'There's nothing but good news, mate. We're all off the hook. The delicatessen, together with Cromwell's office, burned down last night. Nothing left but an empty shell. They're calling it a suspicious fire but Delbert's vanished and all his paperwork has gone up in smoke so there's nothing to find.'

Hearing this, Leo started to laugh and then found that he couldn't stop.

'Leo? Are you hysterical, man? Sounds like you're having a fit.'

Finally, he controlled himself sufficiently to speak. 'You won't believe this, Harry. It's the perfect irony. I just got married to Rosalie — today — so as to keep her safe.'

'You old dog, you! Congratulations. I always knew there was something there — it was only a question of time. What took you so long?'

'It's not like that, Harry — just a marriage of convenience.'

'Yeah, yeah. Look, I have to go. Places to go, people to see. Come and stay with us when you're next in Rome. The missus would like to meet your new bride.' So saying, Harry rang off, leaving Leo staring at the phone almost in disbelief.

He went downstairs in a daze, not quite

ready to mention this turn of events to anyone and he didn't have to as the party was still in full swing. Avoiding the formalities of a normal wedding reception, it was a happy, carefree occasion that didn't run late because they all knew the horses would need their attention in the early hours of the morning. After many remarks heavy with innuendo, everyone went away with a large chunk of wedding cake, leaving Rosalie and Leo at last alone.

15

Leo didn't mention the phone call from Harry until they joined Hannah in the kitchen. Expecting the worst, she made coffee for all of them before sitting down at the table, waiting to hear the news from Italy. Briefly and succinctly, Leo told them.

'So what happens now?' Rosalie said in a small voice, expecting him to say he wanted the marriage annulled.

'I don't know.' Leo wasn't quite able to meet her gaze. 'It's too late to decide anything tonight — perhaps we should talk about it in the morning.' So saying, he yawned and stretched rather theatrically. 'I'm tired out and I'm going to bed,' he announced. 'See you both in the — '

'No, Leo,' Rosalie said softly. 'I'm not going to bed alone.'

'Now just a moment, Rosie — you know very well that's not what I signed up for.'

'Oh but you did, Leo,' Hannah put in. 'I was there, remember. I signed your wedding certificate as one of your witnesses. And I've also taken the liberty of rearranging your room.'

'A liberty indeed, Hannah. Nobody asked you to do that.'

'No? You can't expect your new bride to sleep in your frowsty old bed with your well-worn sheets and pillows. As a wedding present to both of you, I've made it completely fresh, from the mattress up, and I even put on a new bedspread, too.'

'Thank you so much, Hannah.' Rosalie gave her an exuberant hug and a kiss. 'For everything. I appreciate it, even if Leo doesn't. I can't wait to see what you've done for us and we'll both see you in the morning.' And, holding out her hand to Leo, she made it impossible for him to do anything but accept it.

As soon as she was sure they weren't coming back, Hannah found and opened the letter she had from Jake that day. She had saved it to read when she was alone as it was the first time that he'd been in touch since he went away.

Dear Ma,

I expect you'll be surprised to hear from me after all this time but I think of you often and wonder how you're *doing. And Leo, too.*

I'm a lot older and wiser now so I'm wondering — how would you feel if I were to come home? I've had a lot of amazing adventures but it's all been there, done that, and I'm ready to settle down now. I had a girlfriend but the bitch threw me out. As you can see, I'm in Sydney at present but I'm longing to see you again so if you could send me a few hundred dollars for the plane fare . . .

Hannah closed her eyes against incipient tears, unable to read any more. Jake was no son of hers, he was feckless and careless of others as his father had been. She didn't have to be told — he had already spent all her savings and she would be foolish indeed to let him back into her life, bringing all the heartache that went along with it. Jake didn't or couldn't love anyone — people were just grist to his mill, to be used and cast aside.

To make sure she would never be tempted to read it again and without taking note of any address in Sydney, she opened the door of the Aga, pushed in Jake's note and watched it sizzle in the dying embers of the fire.

Upstairs, Leo spent a long time in the bathroom, washing and cleaning his teeth, finding it hard to come to terms with what Hannah had done to his bedroom. It smelled of an expensive room freshener and no longer felt like his own, even the bed looked unfamiliar and new. Hannah had also turned off the overhead lights and decorated the bedside tables with pretty tea-lights in coloured vases. It was a room perfectly set up for a romance that was not going to be.

He stayed in the bathroom as long as he could, wanting to give Rosalie enough time to undress and get into bed. With any luck she'd be tired out herself and have fallen asleep.

Instead, she was sitting up in bed, waiting for him, an old-fashioned vision of loveliness in a vintage nightdress.

'Get into bed, Leo,' she smiled, patting his side of the bed. 'I'm not going to bite.'

Gingerly, he climbed in, staying as far away from her as he could and trying not to look at her peaking nipples, outlined by the flimsy silk of her gown. What was she doing to him? She might as well have been sitting there naked. Obviously, she was waiting for him to do something or say something but his mouth was suddenly dry. Sleep was the last thing on her mind and that would be impossible for either of them now.

'Oh, Leo,' she spoke instead, sensing his embarrassment. 'Don't look so appalled. I'm still me. I didn't suddenly turn into a vampire.'

'Oh, Rosie, I don't think any such thing. You're quite beautiful, of course you are.' He turned towards her, his face inches from her own. 'It's not your fault I'm like this. Not at all. It's me.'

Her eyes flashed fire. 'Don't give me that old 'it's not you, it's me' cliché. It just isn't fair.'

'Nothing about this marriage is fair. It's not fair for you to be tied to a sad old man who doesn't deserve you. And you don't have to — tomorrow we can — '

'Ssh!' Quickly, she placed her fingers across his lips to stem the flow of his words. 'Is that really how you see yourself, Leo? A sad old man? Well, I don't see you that way — not at all. I'm old-fashioned enough to want a man mature enough to take care of me as a wife and the house full of children that I mean to have.'

'A house full of children?' His eyes widened. 'You want that with me?'

'Who else? But only if it's what you want as well.'

'Rosie, it's late and this is emotional stuff. I think we should get some sleep and talk about this again in the morning.'

'OK. I can do that.'

To his relief, she seemed to be composing herself for sleep although she was still facing towards him. He tried closing his own eyes for a moment or two and then opened them, sensing she wasn't asleep. He found her still wide awake and watching him.

'What is it, Rosie? What the hell is it now?'

'Leo, would you kiss me properly just once, please? Before we go to sleep?'

'Really?' He groaned and made to give her a peck on the lips but she surprised him by putting her arms around his neck and pulling him closer, opening her mouth to receive his kiss. To Leo, it felt both unexpected and wonderful; that pliant body pressed close, almost writhing against his own.

From that moment on, he was lost in the throes of a strong desire he could never remember feeling before and he didn't want the kissing to stop. At last the floodgates had opened and all the suppressed desire, the pent-up emotion he had not been allowed to give Mary, was there. He wanted much more than kisses from Rosalie and knew that he had to have her — really have her in every possible way. She had made herself impossible for him to resist.

Rosalie, in turn, felt as if she were embracing a tiger. Leo's body was hard and urgent against her own, he was grazing her face with his stubble as he plundered her mouth and she knew he was about to take a lot more from her than a few kisses. It was too much all at once. She wanted to savour these moments and take some time about it but, lost to passion, he tore the nightgown from her shoulders, breaking the flimsy straps to give full and proper attention to her breasts. Although all these sensations were new, Rosalie started to match his passion with her own. She lifted herself towards him as, groaning with pleasure, she felt herself grow hot and wet in response and parted her legs to accommodate him.

Pinning her arms above her head, he pushed his way in, realizing she was more than ready. Even if she wasn't, he wouldn't have cared. He couldn't have stopped if he'd wanted to and when she cried out softly, either with pain or pleasure, somehow it urged him to push harder than ever.

Finally, the ride was over and they both lay back, panting from their exertions, for the moment unable to speak.

'Oh God, I'm sorry, Rosie,' he said at last. 'I didn't mean to hurt you.'

'If you did, I deserved it,' she said, surprising him by laughing richly — a woman's laugh, no longer that of a girl. 'Too late for an annulment now, Leo. Our marriage has been well and truly consummated and I have the sheets to prove it.'

'You started something and I had to finish it. I just couldn't stop myself,' Leo said. 'And look,' he said, picking up a strap dangling from her shoulder. 'I tore your nightgown.'

'That's what it was for,' she said, leaning over and kissing him again, running her hands through his hair. 'I absolutely intended to drive you crazy.'

'I must have loved you forever but I didn't see it until now,' he said. 'Everything that went before was — well, it was just an illusion.'

He was thinking of Mary and how he had been both dazzled and deceived by her. Ever since they met, Rosalie had always been there for him and she would be the perfect partner to take into the future, sharing his interest in breeding and training good horses.

Looking down at his bride who was now lying sated and asleep in his arms, he counted himself a fortunate man.

We do hope that you have enjoyed reading this large print book.

Did you know that all of our titles are available for purchase?

We publish a wide range of high quality large print books including:
Romances, Mysteries, Classics
General Fiction
Non Fiction and Westerns

Special interest titles available in large print are:
The Little Oxford Dictionary
Music Book
Song Book
Hymn Book
Service Book

Also available from us courtesy of Oxford University Press:
Young Readers' Dictionary
(large print edition)
Young Readers' Thesaurus
(large print edition)

For further information or a free brochure, please contact us at:
Ulverscroft Large Print Books Ltd.,
The Green, Bradgate Road, Anstey,
Leicester, LE7 7FU, England.
Tel: (00 44) 0116 236 4325
Fax: (00 44) 0116 234 0205

RIDING THE STORM

Heather Graves

The Lanigan brothers are consumed by a fierce rivalry: both love the same woman, and both covet the same beautiful racehorse, Hunter's Moon. When Robert is the loser for the second time, he exacts a terrible revenge upon Peter — engineering his death, and acquiring Hunter's Moon for himself . . . Months later, still mourning his father, Peter's son Ryan is orphaned by a cyclone which rages through Queensland, killing his mother and destroying his home and livelihood. Val, Robert's kindly wife, offers him sanctuary in her home in Melbourne. Whilst Ryan detests the idea of living with his uncle, it's his only chance to see his beloved Hunter's Moon again . . .

ON TRACK TO MURDER

Heather Graves

Married at sixteen to a man over thirty years her senior, ten years on Larissa Barton begins to question the decision she made, especially when she discovers that Miles is cheating on her. All the same, she is shocked when Miles is the one to ask for a divorce. After leaving him, Larissa returns to her childhood home; she must rebuild her life with new friends. But Miles is jealous of his wife's new-found happiness, and he begins to use his power and influence to meddle in the lives of the people she loves . . .

INDIGO NIGHTS

Heather Graves

Having both suffered loss, Paige McHugh and Luke Sandford are wary of trusting again. They have a comfortable working relationship as jockey and trainer; Paige knows they've no business to be falling in love, particularly as Luke's fiancée isn't quite his ex. However, after winning the prestigious Golden Slipper in Sydney, their emotions overtake them. But is their relationship doomed? And who is causing trouble for Paige and her grandmother? Who's behind the frightening nocturnal visits to their isolated home? Then the safety of Paige's little son, Marc, is also threatened — can the mystery be solved before tragedy strikes?